THE TRACK OF SAND

Inspector Salvatore Montalbano wakes one morning to find a gruesomely bludgeoned horse carcass in front of his seaside home — but when his men come to investigate, it has disappeared, leaving only a trail in the sand. Soon Rachele Esterman, a beautiful and wealthy equestrian, turns up at police headquarters to report her horse missing; it had been stabled on grounds belonging to Saverio Lo Duca, one of the richest men in Sicily — who, it emerges, lost one of his own horses at the same time. His curiosity piqued, Montalbano takes up the case, but things take a disturbingly personal turn with a series of mysterious break-ins at his house. Who has the inspector upset within the strange, glittering world of horse racing and the Mafia?

THE TRACK OF SAND

TRANSLATED BY STEPHEN SARTARELLI

ANDREA CAMILLERI

ISIS
LARGE
PRINT

First published in Great Britain 2010
by
Picador
an imprint of Pan Macmillan

First Isis Edition
published 2017
by arrangement with
Pan Macmillan
a division of Macmillan Publishers Limited

A catalogue record for this book is available
from the British Library.

ISBN 978-1-78541-315-5 (hb)
ISBN 978-1-78541-321-6 (pb)

Published by
F. A. Thorpe (Publishing)
Anstey, Leicestershire

Set by Words & Graphics Ltd.
Anstey, Leicestershire
Printed and bound in Great Britain by
T. J. International Ltd., Padstow, Cornwall

This book is printed on acid-free paper

CHAPTER
ONE

He opened his eyes and immediately closed them again.

For some time now, he had been sort of refusing to wake up in the morning. It was not, however, to prolong any pleasurable dreams, which he was having fewer and fewer of these days. No, it was a pure and simple desire to remain just a little while longer inside the dark well of sleep, warm and deep, hidden at the very bottom, where it would be impossible for anyone to find him.

But he knew he was irremediably awake. And so, with his eyes still sealed, he started listening to the sound of the sea.

The sound was ever so slight that morning, almost a rustling of leaves, always repeating, always the same, a sign that the surf, coming and going, was breathing calmly. The day therefore promised to be a good one, without wind.

He opened his eyes, looked at the clock. Seven. As he was about to get up, a dream he'd had came back to him, but he could remember only a few confused, disconnected images. An excellent excuse to delay getting up a little longer. Stretching back out, he closed

1

his eyes again, trying to put the scattered snapshots in order.

There was someone beside him in a sort of vast, grassy expanse, a woman, and he now realized that it was Livia, but it wasn't Livia. That is, she had Livia's face, but her body was too big, deformed by a pair of buttocks so huge that she had difficulty walking.

He felt tired, as after a long walk, though he couldn't remember how long they had been walking.

So he asked her: "Is there far to go?"

"Are you tired already? Not even a small child would be worn out so quickly! We're almost there."

The voice was not Livia's. It was coarse, and too shrill.

They took another hundred steps or so and found themselves in front of an open cast-iron gate. The grassy meadow continued on the other side.

What on earth was that gate doing there, if there was no road or house as far as the eye could see? He wanted to ask the woman this, but didn't, not wanting to hear her voice again.

The absurdity of passing through a gate that served no purpose and led to nowhere seemed so ridiculous to him that he stepped aside to walk around it.

"No!" the woman yelled. "What are you doing? That's not allowed! They might get upset!"

Her voice was so shrill it nearly pierced his eardrums. Who were "they"? All the same, he obeyed.

Just past the gate, the landscape changed, turning into a racecourse with a dirt track. But there wasn't a single spectator; the grandstands were empty.

Then he realized he was wearing riding boots with spurs instead of his regular shoes, and that he was dressed exactly like a jockey. He even had a little whip under his arm. *Matre santa*, what did they want from him? He had never ridden a horse in his life! Or rather, yes, once, when he was ten years old and his uncle had taken him to the countryside where —

"Mount me," said the coarse voice.

He turned and looked at the woman.

She was no longer a woman, but sort of a horse. She had got down on all fours, but the hooves over her hands and feet were clearly fake, made out of bone, and indeed, the ones on her feet were slipped on, like slippers.

She was wearing a saddle and bridle.

"Come on, mount me," she repeated.

He mounted and she took off at a gallop like a rocket. *Bumpety bumpety bumpety bumpety bumpety bumpety . . .*

"Stop! Stop!" he cried.

But she only ran faster. At one point he was on the ground, having fallen, with his left foot caught in the stirrup and the horse neighing — no, she was laughing and laughing . . . Then the horse-woman fell forward onto her front legs with a whinny, and, finding himself suddenly free, he ran away.

He couldn't remember anything else, try as he might. He opened his eyes, got out of bed, went to the window, and threw open the shutters.

And the first thing he saw was a horse, lying on its side in the sand, motionless.

For a second he balked. He thought he was still dreaming. Then he realized that the animal on the beach was real. But why had it come to die right in front of his house? Surely when it fell it must have emitted a faint neigh, just enough to set him spinning, in his sleep, the dream of the horse-woman.

He leaned out of the window to have a better look. There wasn't a living soul. The fisherman who set out from those waters every morning in his little boat was now a tiny black dot on the sea. The horse's hooves had left a series of tracks at the edge of the beach, on the hard sand nearest the water, but he couldn't see where they began.

The horse had come from far away.

He hastily slipped on a pair of trousers and a shirt, opened the French windows, crossed the veranda, and stepped down onto the beach.

When he got close to the animal and looked at it, he was overcome with rage.

"Bastards!"

The beast was all bloodied, its head broken open with some sort of iron bar, its whole body bearing the signs of a long, ferocious beating. There were deep, open wounds, pieces of flesh dangling. It was clear that the horse, battered as it was, had managed to escape and run desperately away until it could go no further.

The inspector felt so furious and indignant that had he had one of the horse's killers in his hands at that

4

moment, he would have made him meet the same end. He started following the hoofprints.

Every so often they came to an abrupt halt, and in their place there were signs in the sand indicating that the poor animal had fallen to its knees.

He walked for almost forty-five minutes before reaching the spot where the horse had been bludgeoned.

Here, because of all the frantic stepping and trampling, the surface of the sand had formed a kind of circus ring marked with a confusion of overlapping shoe prints and hoofprints. Scattered around it were three iron bars stained with dried blood, and a long, broken rope, probably used to restrain the beast. The inspector started counting the different shoe prints, which was not easy. He came to the conclusion that four people, at most, had killed the horse. But two others had witnessed the spectacle, keeping still at the edge of the ring and smoking.

He turned back, went into the house, and phoned the station.

"Halloo? Iss izza — "

"Catarella, Montalbano here."

"Ah, Chief! Iss you? Whass wrong, Chief?"

"Is Inspector Augello there?"

"He in't presentable yet."

"Then let me talk to Fazio, if he's there."

Less than a minute passed.

"What can I do for you, Chief?"

"Listen, Fazio, I want you to come here to my place right away, and bring Gallo and Galluzzo with you, if they're there."

"Something up?"

"Yes."

He left the front door to the house open and took a long walk down the beach. The barbaric slaughter of that poor animal had kindled a dull, violent rage in him. He approached the horse again and crouched down for a better look. They had even bludgeoned it in the belly, perhaps when it had reared up. Then he noticed that one of the horseshoes was almost completely detached from the hoof. He lay on the ground, belly down, reached out and touched it. It was held in place by a single nail, which had come halfway out of the hoof. At that moment Fazio, Gallo, and Galluzzo arrived, looked out from the veranda, spotted the inspector, and came down onto the beach. They looked at the horse and asked no questions.

Only Fazio spoke.

"There are some vile people in this world!" he commented.

"Gallo, think you can bring the car down here and then drive it along the beach?" Montalbano asked.

Gallo gave a haughty smile.

"Piece o' cake, Chief."

"Galluzzo, you go with him. I want you to follow the hoofprints. You shouldn't have any trouble finding the spot where they bludgeoned the creature. There are iron bars, cigarette butts, and maybe other things as well. See for yourselves. Then gather everything together very carefully; I want fingerprints taken, DNA tests, the works. Anything that'll help us identify these jokers."

"And then what'll we do? Report them to the Society for the Prevention of Cruelty to Animals?" Fazio asked as the two of them were walking away.

"Why, do you think that's all there is to this affair?"

"No, I don't. I just wanted to make that remark."

"Well, I don't think it's worth repeating. So why did they do it?"

Fazio made a doubtful face.

"Could be some kind of revenge on the horse's owner."

"Maybe. And that's all?"

"No. There's something more likely. I've heard talk . . ."

"Of what?"

"Of a clandestine horse-racing circuit in Vigàta."

"And you think this horse was killed as a consequence of something that happened in those circles?"

"What else could it be? All we gotta do now is wait for the consequences of this consequence, which surely will come."

"But maybe it's better if we can prevent this consequence from happening, no?" said Montalbano.

"That'd be better, sure, but it ain't gonna be easy."

"Well, let's begin by saying that before killing the horse, they must have stolen it."

"Are you kidding, Chief? Nobody's gonna report the stolen horse. It would be like coming to us and saying, 'I'm one of the organizers of the illegal horse races.'"

7

"Is it a really big deal?"

"Millions and millions of euros in bets, they say."

"And who's behind it?"

"I've heard the name Michele Prestia mentioned."

"And who's he?"

"Some nitwit, Chief, about fifty years old. Who up until last year worked as an accountant for a construction firm."

"But this doesn't seem to me like the work of some nitwit accountant."

"Of course not, Chief. Prestia's just a front man, in fact."

"For whom?"

"Nobody knows."

"You have to try to find out."

"I'll try."

When they were back in the house, Fazio went into the kitchen to make coffee and Montalbano called City Hall to inform them that there was a horse's carcass on the beach at Marinella.

"Is it your horse?"

"No."

"Let's be clear about this, sir."

"Why, is there something unclear about what I said?"

"No, it's just that sometimes people say the animal's not theirs because they don't want to pay the removal fee."

"I told you it's not my horse."

"OK, we'll take your word for it. Do you know whose it is?"

"No."

"OK, we'll take your word for it. Do you know what it died of?"

Montalbano weighed his options and decided not to tell the clerk anything.

"No, I don't. I just saw the dead body out of my window."

"So you didn't see it die."

"Obviously."

"OK, we'll take your word for it," said the clerk, who then started humming "Tu che a Dio spiegasti l'ali".

A funeral lament for the horse? A kind homage from City Hall, as a way to join in the mourning?

"Well?" said Montalbano.

"I was thinking," said the clerk.

"What's there to think about?"

"I have to work out whose job it is to remove the carcass."

"Isn't it yours?"

"It would be ours if it's an Article 11, but if, on the other hand, it's an Article 23, it's the job of the provincial Office of Hygiene."

"Listen, given the fact that you've taken my word for everything thus far, I advise you to keep doing so. Because I assure you that either you come within fifteen minutes and take it away, or I'm going to —"

"And who are you, may I ask?"

"I'm Inspector Montalbano."

The clerk's tone immediately changed.

"It's definitely an Article 11, Inspector, I'm sure of it."

Montalbano felt like teasing him.

"So it's up to you to remove it?"

"It certainly is."

"Are you absolutely sure?"

The clerk became worried.

"Why are you asking me — "

"I wouldn't want the people at the Office of Hygiene to take it the wrong way. You know how prickly these questions of jurisdiction can be . . . I say this for your sake. I wouldn't want —"

"No need to worry, Inspector. It's an Article 11. Somebody will be there in half an hour. No trouble at all. My respects, sir."

Montalbano and Fazio drank coffee in the kitchen while waiting for Gallo and Galluzzo to return. The inspector then took a shower, shaved, and got dressed, changing his shirt and trousers, which had got soiled. When he went back into the dining room he saw Fazio on the veranda, talking to two men dressed like astronauts who had just stepped out of the space shuttle.

On the beach was a little Fiat Fiorino van with its rear doors closed. The horse was no longer visible; apparently it had been loaded inside.

"Hey, Chief, can you come here a minute?" asked Fazio.

"Here I am. Good morning, gentlemen."

"Good morning," said one of the astronauts.

The other gave him a dirty look over the top of his mask.

"They can't find the carcass," said Fazio, flummoxed.

"What do you mean they can't ...?" said Montalbano, upset. "But it was right here!"

"We've looked everywhere and haven't seen anything," said the more sociable of the two.

"What is this, some kind of practical joke? You wanna play games or something?" the other said menacingly.

"Nobody's joking here," Fazio snapped back at the man, who was beginning to get on his nerves. "And watch your tongue."

The other was about to reply, but thought better of it.

Montalbano stepped down from the veranda and went to examine the spot where the carcass had been. The others followed him.

In the sand were the footprints of five or six different shoes and two parallel tracks from the wheels of a cart.

Meanwhile the two astronauts got back into their van and drove off without saying goodbye.

"They stole it while we were having coffee," said the inspector. "They loaded it onto a hand-drawn cart."

"About two miles from here, near Montereale, there's about ten shanties with illegal immigrants living in them," said Fazio. "They're gonna have a feast tonight. They're gonna eat horsemeat."

At that moment they saw their car returning.

"We took everything we could find," said Galluzzo.

"And what did you find?"

"Three bars, a piece of rope, eleven cigarette butts of two different brands, and an empty Bic lighter," Galluzzo replied.

"Let's do this," said Montalbano. "You, Gallo, go to forensics and give them the bars and the lighter. You, Galluzzo, take the rope and butts and bring them to my office. Thanks for everything. We'll meet back at the station. I've got a couple of private phone calls to make."

Gallo looked doubtful.

"What's wrong?"

"What am I supposed to ask forensics to do?"

"To take fingerprints."

Gallo looked more doubtful than ever.

"And if they ask me what it's about, what do I say? That we're investigating the murder of a horse? They'll throw me out of there on my arse!"

"Tell them there was a fight with several wounded and we're trying to identify the assailants."

Left alone, he went inside, took off his shoes and socks, rolled up his trousers, and went back onto the beach.

This idea of immigrants stealing the horse to eat it didn't convince him in the least. How long had they been in the kitchen, he and Fazio, drinking coffee and chatting? Half an hour, max.

So, in half an hour the immigrants had the time to spot the horse, run two miles back to their shanties, get a cart, return to the beach, load it on the cart, and roll it away?

It wasn't possible.

Unless they had spotted the carcass at the crack of dawn, before he opened the window, and then had returned with the cart, seen him next to the horse, and hidden nearby, waiting for the right moment.

Some fifty yards down the beach, the tracks made a turn and headed inland, where there was a concrete esplanade full of cracks, which was how it had always looked to the inspector since he first moved to Marinella. The esplanade provided easy entry onto the provincial road.

Wait a second, he said to himself. *Let's think about this.*

Yes, the immigrants could move the cart more easily, and more quickly, on the provincial road than on the sand. But was it really such a good idea to let themselves be seen by all the passing cars? What if one of them belonged to the police or the carabinieri?

They would surely be stopped and made to answer a lot of questions. And quite possibly a repatriation order would come out of it all.

No, they weren't that stupid.

And so?

There was another possible explanation.

Namely, that the people who stole the horse were not illegals, but legals and then some. That is, from Vigàta.

Or the surrounding area.

So why did they do it? To recover the carcass and get rid of it.

Perhaps the whole thing had gone as follows: the horse escapes and someone chases after it to finish it off. But he is forced to stop because there are people on the beach, maybe even the morning fisherman, who could become dangerous witnesses. So he returns and informs the boss. The boss decides they absolutely have to get the carcass back, and he organizes the business with the cart. But then he, Montalbano, wakes up and throws a wrench into the boss's plans.

The people who stole the dead horse were the same ones who killed it.

Yes, that must be exactly the way it went.

And at the side of the provincial road, right where the esplanade abutted it, there had surely been a van or truck ready for loading the horse and cart.

No, illegal immigrants had nothing to do with this.

CHAPTER
TWO

Galluzzo set down on the inspector's desk a large plastic bag with the rope in it, along with another, smaller bag with the cigarette butts.

"You said there were two brands?"

"Yeah, Chief. Marlboro and Philip Morris, with the double filter."

Very common. He had hoped for some rare brand smoked by no more than five people in Vigàta.

"You take all this," Montalbano said to Fazio, "and take good care of it. It may turn out to be useful to us later."

"Let's hope so," said Fazio, not very convinced.

At that moment a high-powered bomb seemed to explode behind the door, which flew open and crashed against the wall, revealing Catarella sprawled out on the floor with two envelopes in his hand.

"I's bringin' the post," said Catarella, "but I slipped."

The three men in the office tried to collect themselves after the scare. They looked at one another and immediately understood. They had only two options: proceed to Catarella's summary execution, or say nothing.

They chose the second and said nothing.

"Sorry to repeat myself, but I don't think it's gonna be so easy to identify the horse's owner," said Fazio.

"We should have at least taken some photographs of it," said Galluzzo.

"Isn't there some sort of registry for horses, like there is for cars?" asked Montalbano.

"I don't know," replied Fazio. "And then we don't even know what kind of horse it was."

"What do you mean?"

"I mean we don't know if it was a draught horse, a stud horse, a show horse, a racehorse . . ."

"Horses are banded," said Catarella, under his breath, still outside, envelopes in hand, since the inspector had never told him to come in.

Montalbano, Fazio, and Galluzzo looked at him, stupefied.

"What did you say?" asked Montalbano.

"Me? I din't say nothin'!" said Catarella, frightened at having made the mistake of opening his mouth.

"Yes you did! You said something just now! What did you say horses were?"

"I said they was banded, Chief."

"And how are they banded?"

Catarella looked doubtful.

"They's banded wit' whatever they's banded wit', Chief, I dunno, mebbe wit' bands."

"All right, give me the post and get out of here."

Mortified, Catarella put the letters on the desk and went out with his eyes downcast. In the doorway he nearly collided with Mimì Augello, who was rushing in.

"Sorry I'm late, but I had to lend a hand with the kid, who — "

"You're forgiven."

"And what are those exhibits there?" Mimì asked, seeing the rope and cigarette butts on the desk.

"A horse was bludgeoned to death," said Montalbano. And he told him the whole story.

"You know anything about horses?" he asked when he had finished.

Mimì laughed. "All they have to do is look at me to scare me, just to give you an idea."

"But isn't there anyone here at the station who knows anything about them?"

"I really don't think so," said Fazio.

"Then we'll drop it for the moment. How did the business with Pepè Rizzo turn out?"

This was a case that Mimì had been working on. Pepè Rizzo was suspected of being the wholesaler for all the *vocumprà* in the province, supplying them with everything in the world that could be faked, from Rolexes and Lacoste alligator shirts to CDs and DVDs. Mimì had found the warehouse, and the previous day he had succeeded in getting a search warrant from the prosecutor. Upon hearing the question, Mimì started laughing.

"We found everything but the kitchen sink, Salvo! There were brand-name shirts that looked so much like the real thing, it made my heart —"

"Stop right there!" the inspector ordered him.

Everyone looked at him in bafflement.

"Catarella!"

The inspector's shout was so loud that it blew Fazio's exhibits, which he was gathering together, off the desktop.

Catarella arrived at a run and, slipping again in front of the door, managed to grab onto the jamb to keep from falling.

"Catarella, listen carefully."

"Atcha service, Chief."

"When you said that horses were banded, did you mean that they're banded by their owners?"

"'Assit, Chief, 'ass azzackly what I mint."

And that was why it was so important for the killers to recover the carcass!

"Thanks, you can go now." Then, turning to the others: "Understand?"

"No," said Augello.

"Catarella has reminded us, in his own way, that horses are often heat-branded with the initials of the owner or the stable. Our horse must have fallen on the side with the brand, which is why I didn't see it. And, to be honest, it never even crossed my mind to look for it."

Fazio turned slightly pensive.

"I'm beginning to think that maybe the illegal aliens — "

"Have nothing to do with this," Montalbano completed his sentence. "After you all left this morning, I became convinced of it. The cart tracks did not lead all the way to their shanties; after some fifty yards or so, they turned towards the provincial road.

18

Where there must certainly have been a truck waiting for them."

"From what I can gather," Mimì intervened, "it looks like they got rid of the only lead we had."

"And that's why it won't be easy to identify the owner," Fazio concluded.

"Barring some stroke of luck," said Mimì.

Montalbano noticed that for some time now, Fazio seemed to lack confidence, as if finding things more and more difficult. Maybe the years were beginning to weigh on him, too.

But they were wrong, quite wrong, to think it would be so difficult to identify the horse's owner.

At lunchtime the inspector went to Enzo's, but he didn't do justice to the dishes he was served. In his head he still had the scene of the bludgeoned horse lying on the sand. At one point he came out with a question that surprised him.

What's it like to eat horsemeat?

I've never tasted it. They say it's sort of sweet.

As he had eaten very little, he felt no need to take his customary stroll along the jetty. When he returned to the office, there were papers for him to sign.

At four o'clock the telephone rang.

"Chief, that'd be a lady named Esther."

"She didn't give you her full name?"

"Yessir, she did, an' iss what I juss tol' you."

"So she's Miss or Mrs Esther?"

"Zackly, Chief. An' her lass name is Man."

Esther Mann. He'd never heard of her.

"Did she tell you what it was about?"

"Nossir."

"Well, have her talk to Fazio or Augello."

"They ain't presentable, Chief."

"All right, then, send her in."

"My name is Esterman, Rachele Esterman," said a fortyish woman in jacket and jeans, tall, with blonde hair falling onto her shoulders, blue eyes, long legs, and a solid, athletic body. In short, the way one imagines the Valkyries looked.

"Make yourself comfortable, signora."

She sat down and crossed her legs. How was it that her legs looked even longer when crossed?

"What can I do for you?" he asked.

"I'm here to report the disappearance of a horse."

Montalbano gave a start in his chair, but concealed the movement by feigning a coughing fit.

"I can see you're a smoker," said Rachele, gesturing towards the ashtray and packet of cigarettes on the desk.

"Yes, but I don't think my cough has got anything —"

"I wasn't referring to your cough, which, in any case, sounded clearly faked. I meant that since you smoke, I can smoke, too."

And she pulled a packet out of her handbag.

"Well, actually . . ."

"You mean it's prohibited here? Do you feel like transgressing a little, for as long as it takes to smoke a cigarette? We can open the window afterwards."

She stood up, went to close the door, which had been left open, sat down again, stuck a cigarette between her lips, and leaned towards the inspector so he could light it.

"So, tell me," she said, blowing the smoke out of her nose.

"I'm sorry, but it's you who came here to tell *me* something . . ."

"At first. But when you reacted so clumsily to my words, I realized you had already been informed of the disappearance. Am I right?"

The bright-eyed goddess could probably see flutters in the nostril hairs of anyone in front of her. He might as well lay his cards on the table.

"Yes, you are. But shall we proceed in an orderly fashion?"

"Let's."

"Do you live here?"

"I've been in Montelusa for three days, staying at a friend's house."

"If you're living in Montelusa, even temporarily, then by law you should file your report in — "

"But the horse had been put in the care of someone from Vigàta."

"What's the name?"

"Saverio Lo Duca."

Shit. Saverio Lo Duca was easily one of the richest men in Sicily and had a stable in Vigàta. With four or five prized horses he kept just for the fun of it, for the pleasure of owning them. He never entered them in shows or races. Every so often he would come into town and spend an entire day with them. He had powerful friends, and dealings with him were always a pain, because there was always the danger that one would say the wrong thing and piss outside the urinal.

"Let me get this straight. You brought your horse along with you when you came to Montelusa?"

Rachele Esterman gave him a puzzled look.

"Of course. I had to."

"And why's that?"

"Because the day after tomorrow, at Fiacca, there's going to be the ladies' race, the one organized every two years by the Barone Piscopo di San Militello."

"Ah, yes."

It was a lie. He had never heard of this race.

"When did you realize the horse had been stolen?"

"Me? I didn't realize anything. I received a phone call in Montelusa at dawn this morning from the chief hand at Chichi's stable."

"I don't think — "

"I'm sorry. Chichi is Saverio Lo Duca."

"But if you were informed of the disappearance first thing this morning — "

"Why did I wait so long to report it?"

She was smart. But her way of finishing his sentences got on his nerves.

"Because my sorrel — "

"Your what? Is that the horse's name? Like Julien Sorel?"

She laughed heartily, throwing her head backwards.

"You really don't know the first thing about horses, do you?"

"Well . . ."

"Horses with chestnut coats are called sorrels. As I was saying, my horse — whose name, as it happens, is Super — has a habit of running away from time to time, making us go out and look for him. So they looked for him but then phoned me around three to tell me they hadn't found him. And I concluded that he hadn't run away."

"I see. You don't think that in the meantime they — "

"They would have called me on the mobile."

She had him light another cigarette.

"And now give me the bad news."

"What makes you surmise that — "

"Inspector, you've been very shrewd. With the excuse that we should proceed in an orderly fashion, you've avoided answering my question. You're stalling. And this can mean only one thing. Has he been kidnapped? Should I expect a demand for a great deal of money?"

"Is he worth a lot?"

"A fortune. He's a thoroughbred English racehorse."

What to do? Better tell her everything, in small steps, since he would have to come out with it in the end anyway.

"He hasn't been kidnapped."

Rachele Esterman leaned back stiffly in her chair, suddenly pale.

"How can you know that? Have you spoken to anyone at the stable?"

"No."

Looking at her, Montalbano felt as if he could hear the gears whirring in her brain.

"Is he . . . dead?"

"Yes."

The woman pulled the ashtray towards her, took the cigarette out of her mouth, and extinguished it with great care.

"Was he run over by — "

"No."

She must not have understood the meaning of this at once, because she repeated the word "no" several times, under her breath, to herself.

Then she suddenly understood.

"Was he killed?"

"Yes."

Without saying a word, she got up, went over to the window, opened it, leaned out with her elbows on the sill. Every so often her shoulders heaved. She was silently crying.

The inspector let her get it out of her system, then went and stood next to her. She was still crying, so he pulled a packet of paper tissues from his jacket pocket and handed it to her.

He then went and filled a glass with some water from a bottle he kept on a filing cabinet, and handed it to her. Rachele drank it all.

"Would you like some more?"

"No, thank you."

They returned to their places. Rachele appeared calm again, but Montalbano feared the questions that were sure to come. Such as: "How was he killed?"

Now, there was a difficult question! But instead of continuing this question-and-answer session, wasn't it perhaps better for him to tell her the whole story from the moment he had opened his bedroom window?

"Please listen to me," he began.

"No," said Rachele.

"You don't want to listen to me?"

"No. I already understand. Do you realize you're sweating?"

He hadn't noticed. Perhaps she should be enrolled in the police force. She didn't miss a thing.

"So what? Is that supposed to mean something?"

"It means they must have killed him in some horrible way. And it's hard for you to tell me. Am I right?"

"Yes."

"Could I see him?"

"That's not possible."

"Why not?"

"Because after they killed him, they took him away."

"For what purpose?"

Indeed, for what purpose?

"Well, we guessed that they removed the carcass" — the word must have stung her, because she briefly closed her eyes — "to prevent us from seeing his brand."

"He wasn't branded."

"Which would have let us track down his owner. But that has proved to be an erroneous surmise, since you have come to report his disappearance."

"But if they thought I would come and report it, what need was there to take him away? I doubt they're planning to put him in my bed."

Montalbano felt at sea. What was this about her bed?

"Could you explain what you mean by that?"

"Haven't you seen *The Godfather*, where they put the horse's head in the movie producer's — "

"Ah, yes."

And why, in the film, had they put the horse's head in the producer's bed? Then he remembered.

"But have you, by any chance, been made an offer you can't refuse?"

She gave a strained smile.

"Oh, I've had a lot of those. And to some I've said yes, to others I've said no. But there's never been any need to slaughter a horse."

"Have you been in these parts before?"

"The last time was two years ago, for the same reason. I live in Rome."

"Are you married?"

"Yes and no."

"Your relationship with —"

"My relationship with my husband is excellent. Fraternal, I'd say. And, anyway, I think Gianfranco would sooner commit suicide than kill a horse."

"Do you have any idea why anyone would want to do such a thing to you?"

"The only one I can think of would be to eliminate me from tomorrow's race, which I would surely have won. But that would seem a bit excessive."

She stood up. Montalbano did likewise.

"Thank your for your courtesy," she said.

"Aren't you going to file a report?"

"Now that he's dead, it doesn't matter any more."

"Are you going back to Rome?"

"No. I'll be going to Fiacca anyway, the day after tomorrow. And I've decided to stay a few more days after that. I would like it if you could keep me informed, especially if you find anything out."

"I'm hoping to do just that. Where can I reach you?"

"Let me give you my mobile number."

The inspector jotted it down on a sheet of paper that he put in his jacket pocket.

"In any case," she continued, "you can always call me at the home of my friend who's putting me up."

"What's the phone number?"

"I think you know it already. She's Ingrid Sjostrom."

CHAPTER
THREE

"And so, just like that, Rachele Esterman has sent all our wonderful hypotheses down the tubes," Montalbano concluded, finishing his account of their meeting.

"While leaving all our problems the same as they were before," said Augello.

"First of all, why did they kidnap and kill the horse of an outsider?" Fazio asked.

"Well," the inspector cut in, "it's possible they have no gripe with her, but with Saverio Lo Duca."

"But then they would have grabbed and killed one of his horses," Mimì objected.

"Maybe they didn't know that the horse didn't belong to Lo Duca. Or else maybe they knew perfectly well and killed it precisely because it didn't belong to Lo Duca."

"I don't follow," said Augello.

"Say there are people who want to do harm to Lo Duca. To ruin his image. If they kill one of his horses, the news probably won't make it out of the province. But if they kill the horse of a woman from his social circle, a horse in his care, then when she goes back to Rome she'll tell everyone what happened, which will put a blot on his reputation. We all know that Lo Duca boasts high and low that he is untouchable and has the respect of everyone, including the Mafia. Does that make sense to you?"

"It makes sense," said Mimì.

"Your argument sounds reasonable enough," Fazio admitted. "But it seems a bit too roundabout to me."

"Could be," Montalbano admitted. "And, second, why did they come back for the carcass, taking a very grave risk?"

"Every idea we've had so far has turned out to be totally wrong. And, to be honest, at the moment I can't come up with any other hypotheses," said Mimì.

"How about you, Fazio? Any ideas?"

"Nah," said Fazio, dejected.

"Well, then, we'll stop right there," said Montalbano. "As soon as somebody has another brilliant idea — "

"Wait a second," Mimì butted in. "Mrs Esterman had second thoughts about reporting the crime and decided it was pointless. So what I'd like to know is: what do we base our next move on?"

"We base our next move on one thing, Mimì, which I'll tell you in a moment. But first I must ask you a question. Do you agree that this sort of thing can have grave consequences?"

"Well, yes."

"So, our next move will be based, unofficially, of course, on the desire to prevent, however we can, any possible reaction. By whom? We don't know. How? We don't know. Where? We don't know. When? We don't know. If you want to take yourself out of the game because there are too many unknowns, you have only to tell me."

"Actually, I think unknowns are fun."

"Then I'm glad to have you on board, Mimi. Fazio, do you know where Lo Duca keeps his horses?"

"Yessir. At Monserrato, near the village of Columba."

"Have you ever been there before?"

"No."

"Then I want you to go there early tomorrow morning, have a look round, and also try to find out who works there. Would it be easy for one or more people to get in and steal a horse? Or did they need accomplices on the inside? And who sleeps there at night? Is it only the caretaker? In short, try to find something you think could serve as a starting point."

"And what about me?" asked Augello.

"Do you know who Michele Prestia is?"

"No. Who is he?"

"A dim-witted former accountant who serves as the front man for the organizers of clandestine horse races. Get Fazio to fill you in on what he already knows about him and then carry on by yourself."

"All right. But can you tell me what the clandestine horse races have to do with this?"

"I don't know if they've got anything to do with it or not, but it's better if we leave no stone unturned."

"Could I say something, Chief?" Fazio interjected.

"Go ahead."

"Wouldn't it be better if Augello and I switched jobs? Because, you see, I know some people who are close to Prestia who — "

30

"You OK with that, Mimì?"

"Makes no difference to me, Salvo," said Augello.

"All right then, I wish you both a very pleasant eve — "

"Wait a second," said Mimì, "sorry to be a spoilsport, but I'd like to make an observation."

"Speak."

"We may be making a mistake to take everything Mrs Esterman told us as the gospel truth."

"What do you mean?"

"Salvo, she came in here and told us that there was no reason in the world why anyone would kill her horse and so on and so forth. But that's only what *she* says. And we gobbled it up like little children. How do we know if it's really true?"

"I see what you're getting at. You think we might do well to learn a little more about the beautiful Signora Rachele, right?"

"Right."

"OK, Mimì. I'll take care of that end of things."

Before heading home, he phoned Ingrid.

"Hello, is this the Sjostrom home?"

"Z gahtz de wrang nomba."

Where on earth did Ingrid dig up these housekeepers?

He checked the number, which he had dialled from memory. It was correct.

Perhaps he'd been wrong to use Ingrid's maiden name. It was unlikely the housekeeper knew it. But

what was her married name? He couldn't remember.
He dialled again.

"Hello? I'd like to speak with Signora Ingrid, please."

"Da ziniuora zinnit ere."

"An doo noze win zhe be baak?"

"Donoze, donoze."

He hung up. He dialled her mobile number.

"*The number of the person . . .*"

He cursed the saints and let it drop.

As he was inserting the key into the lock he heard the
phone ringing. He opened the door and ran to pick it
up.

"Were you looking for me?"

It was Ingrid.

"Yes. I need — "

"You only call me when you need something. You
never ask me out for a candle-lit dinner, never mind the
inevitable conclusion. Just for the pleasure of being
together."

"You know perfectly well that's not true."

"Unfortunately, it's just as I say. What do you need
this time? Consolation? Assistance? An accomplice?"

"Nothing like that at all. I want you to tell me about
your friend Rachele. Is she there with you?"

"No, she's dining in Fiacca tonight with the
organizers of the horse race. I didn't feel like going. Did
you find her attractive?"

"It's not a private matter."

"My, my, how formal we've suddenly become! Well,
just so you know, when Rachele got back she did

nothing but talk about you. About how gracious you are, how understanding, friendly, even handsome, which I think is going a bit too far . . . When do you want to get together?"

"Whenever you like."

"What would you say if I came to Marinella?"

"Right now?"

"Why not? What did Adelina make for you?"

"I haven't checked yet."

"Go and look and then lay the table on the veranda. I'm very hungry. I'll be there in half an hour."

A bowl stuffed with so much caponata that it overflowed. Six mullets in a *cipuddrata*. More than enough for two. Wine, he had. He laid the table outside. It was chilly, but there wasn't even a hint of wind. Just to be sure, he went and checked if he still had any whisky. There was only about two fingers left in the bottle. Dinner with Ingrid was inconceivable without a well-irrigated finale. He dropped everything and got in his car.

At the Marinella Bar he bought two bottles, for which they made him pay four times the normal price. As he turned onto the small road that led home, he saw Ingrid's powerful red car. But she wasn't there. He called her name, but she didn't answer. He guessed she'd probably gone down to the beach, circled around the house, and entered through the veranda doors.

He opened the door, but Ingrid did not come to greet him. He called out.

"I'm in here," he heard her answer from the bedroom.

He put the bottles on the table and went into the bedroom, where he saw her crawling out from under the bed.

"What are you doing?" he asked, confused.

"I was hiding."

"You want to play hide-and-seek?"

Only then did he notice that Ingrid was pale and that her hands were trembling a little.

"What on earth happened?"

"When I got here I rang the doorbell, and when you didn't answer I decided to come in through the veranda. But as soon as I turned the corner I saw two men come out of the house and leave. So I got worried and went inside, thinking that . . . Then I realized they might come back, so I hid. Have you got any whisky?"

"As much as you want."

In the living room he opened a bottle and half-filled a glass for her. She gulped it down.

"That's better."

"Did you get a good look at them?"

"No, just a glimpse. I stepped back immediately."

"Were they armed?"

"I couldn't say."

"Come."

He led her out onto the veranda.

"Which way did they go?"

Ingrid looked doubtful.

"I don't know. When I stuck my head back out a few minutes later, they were already gone, vanished."

"Strange. There's even some moonlight. You should at least have seen two shadows running away."

"No, there wasn't anyone."

So did that mean they had hidden nearby and were waiting for him to return?

"Wait here just one minute," he said to Ingrid.

"Not on your life. I'm coming with you."

Montalbano went out with Ingrid practically glued to his back, took his pistol out of the glove compartment of his car, and put it in his pocket.

"Is your car locked?" he asked.

"No."

"Lock it."

"You lock it," she said, handing him the keys. "But check first and make sure there's nobody hiding inside."

Montalbano looked inside the car, locked it, and they went back indoors.

"You were really scared just now. I've never seen you — "

"You know, when those two left and I went inside and started calling you and you didn't answer, I thought they had . . ."

She stopped, threw her arms around him, and kissed him on the mouth.

Returning her kiss, Montalbano realized the evening was heading down a dangerous path. So he gave her a couple of friendly knocks on the shoulder.

She got the message and let go.

"Who do you think they were?" she asked.

"I haven't the foggiest idea. Maybe some petty thieves who saw me go out and — "

"Oh, stop telling me nonsense you don't even believe yourself!"

"I assure you that — "

"How could these burglars have known there wasn't somebody else in the house? And why didn't they steal anything?"

"You didn't allow them enough time."

"But they never even saw me!"

"Yes, but they heard you ring the doorbell and call me . . . Come on, Adelina has cooked us — "

"I'm afraid to eat outside, on the veranda."

"Why?"

"You would be an easy target."

"Come on, Ingrid . . ."

"Well, then, why did you get your gun?"

She wasn't entirely wrong, when you came right down to it. But he wanted to calm her down.

"Listen, Ingrid, I've been living in Marinella for years and years, and no one has ever come to my house with bad intentions."

"There's always a first time for everything."

Once again, she wasn't entirely wrong.

"Where would you like to eat?"

"In the kitchen. Bring everything in and then close the French windows. Even though I've lost my appetite."

Her appetite returned after two glasses of whisky.

36

They polished off the caponata and divided the mullets evenly, three each.

"When does the interrogation begin?" asked Ingrid.

"Here in the kitchen? Let's go into the living room, where we can relax on the couch."

They brought along a bottle of wine they'd barely begun, as well as the bottle of whisky, already half empty. They sat down on the sofa, but then Ingrid got up again, pulled up a chair, and rested her legs on it. Montalbano set flame to a cigarette.

"Fire away," said Ingrid.

"What I'd like to know about your friend is — "

"Why?"

"Why do I want to know? Because I don't know anything about her."

"So why do you want to know more about her if you're not interested in her as a woman?"

"I'm interested in her as a police inspector."

"What has she done?"

"She hasn't done anything. But as you probably know, her horse was killed, and in a rather barbaric fashion."

"How?"

"Bludgeoned to death with iron bars. But don't tell anyone, not even your friend."

"No, I won't tell anyone. But how did you find out?"

"I saw it with my own eyes. The horse came here to die, right outside the veranda."

"Really? Tell me about it."

"There's nothing to tell. I woke up, opened the window, and saw it lying there."

"All right, but why do you want to know more about Rachele?"

"Since your friend claims not to have any enemies, I am compelled by logic to think that the horse was killed to spite Lo Duca."

"So?"

"I have to know if this is actually the case. How long have you known her?"

"Six years."

"How did you meet?"

Ingrid started laughing.

"Do you really want to know?"

"I'd say so."

"We met in Palermo, at the Igea Hotel. It was five o'clock in the afternoon, and I was in bed with a certain Walter. We had forgotten to lock the door, and she burst in like a banshee. I didn't know Walter had another woman. Stumbling to put his clothes back on, Walter managed to escape. So she pounced on me, as I was sitting there petrified in bed, and tried to strangle me. Luckily two clients who were walking by in the corridor came to my rescue."

"And after this fine start, how did you end up becoming friends?"

"That evening, as I was eating alone in the hotel restaurant, she came and sat down at my table. She apologized to me. We chatted awhile and agreed that Walter was an idiot and a coward. We took a liking to each other and became friends. And there you have it."

"Has she come to see you in Montelusa before?"

"Yes. And not only for the horse race in Fiacca."

"Have you introduced her to many people?"

"Practically all my friends. And she's met others on her own. For example, she's got a circle of friends in Fiacca whom I don't know."

"Has she had any affairs?"

"Not with any of my friends, no. But I wouldn't know what she's been up to in Fiacca."

"She doesn't talk to you about it?"

"She once made vague mention of a certain Guido."

"Does she sleep with him?"

"I couldn't say. She describes him as a sort of *cavalier servente*."

"But haven't any of your male friends tried their luck with her?"

"Almost all of them, as far as that goes."

"And among these 'almost all', was there anyone who tried harder than the rest?"

"Well, Mario Giacco."

"Isn't it possible that, perhaps, without your knowing — "

"That Rachele has been with him? It's possible, though I don't — "

"And couldn't it be possible that Giacco, to avenge himself for having been rejected by her, arranged for the horse to be killed?"

Ingrid did not hesitate.

"I would absolutely rule that out, without any doubt. Mario's an engineer, and he's been in Egypt for the past year. He works for an oil company."

"It was a stupid conjecture, I know. And what sort of relationship does she have with Lo Duca?"

"I have no idea what her relations with Lo Duca are."

"But if she put her horse in his care, they must be friends. Do you know Lo Duca?"

"I do, but I find him unbearable."

"Has Rachele ever talked to you about him?"

"A few times. And pretty indifferently, I'd say. I don't think there's been anything between them. Unless Rachele wants to keep their relationship a secret from me."

"Has she ever done that before?"

"Well, based on your conjectures . . ."

"Do you know if Lo Duca is in Montelusa at the moment?"

"He arrived today, after hearing about the horse."

"Is Esterman her maiden name?"

"No, it's Gianfranco's, her husband's. Her family name is Anselmi del Bosco. She's an aristocrat."

"She told me her relationship with her husband is only 'fraternal'. Why doesn't she divorce him?"

"Divorce him? Are you serious? Gianfranco is as Catholic as they come. He goes to Mass, he goes to confession, he's got some sort of fancy job at the Vatican . . . He would never divorce. I don't even think they're officially separated."

She laughed again, but it wasn't a very happy laugh.

"Basically, she's in the same situation as me . . . Listen, I'm going for a pee, and while I'm away, you should open that other bottle of whisky."

40

She stood up, lurching first to the left, then to the right. Regaining her balance, she headed off unsteadily. Without noticing, they had drunk a whole bottle.

CHAPTER
FOUR

Things ended the same as they had all the other times.

When there were scarcely four fingers of whisky remaining in the second bottle, and they had talked about everything except Rachele Esterman, Ingrid said she felt sleepy and had to go to bed immediately.

"I'll drive you back to Montelusa. You're in no condition to drive."

"And I suppose you are?"

Indeed, the inspector's head was spinning a little.

"Ingrid, I only need to wash my face and I'm ready."

"I, on the other hand, am more inclined to take a shower and slip into bed."

"Into my bed?"

"What other beds are there? I'll be quick," she continued, thick-tongued.

"Listen, Ingrid, it's not — "

"C'mon, Salvo. What's got into you? It certainly won't be the first time. And anyway, you know how much I like sleeping chastely beside you."

Chastely, hah! He alone knew how dearly he had to pay for that chastity: not a wink of sleep, getting up in the middle of the night to take emergency cold showers . . .

"OK, but, you see —"

"And besides, it's so erotic!"

"Ingrid, I am not a saint!"

"That's precisely what I'm counting on," she said, laughing and getting up from the couch.

He woke up late the following morning, with a bit of a headache. He had drunk too much. All that was left of Ingrid was her scent on the sheets and pillow.

He glanced at his watch. Almost nine-thirty. Maybe Ingrid had something to do in Montelusa and had let him sleep. But why hadn't Adelina arrived yet?

Then he remembered that it was Saturday, and on Saturdays she didn't arrive until around noon, after she had done her shopping for the week.

He got up, went into the kitchen, prepared a pot of strong coffee, went into the dining room, opened the French windows, and stepped out onto the veranda.

The day looked like a photograph. Not a breath of wind, everything perfectly still, illuminated by a sun particularly careful not to leave anything in shade. There wasn't even any surf.

He went back inside and immediately noticed his pistol on the table.

Strange. What was it doing —

Then, all at once, he remembered the previous evening and what a frightened Ingrid told him: that two men had entered the house after he went out to the Marinella Bar to buy whisky.

He remembered that he always kept an envelope in the drawer of the nightstand with two or three hundred euros in it, the money he would need for the week, which he would withdraw from the cash machine and put in his pocket. He went and checked the drawer. The envelope was in its place, with all its money inside.

The coffee had bubbled up. He drank two cups, one after the other, and resumed looking around the house to see if anything was missing.

After half an hour of this, he decided that apparently nothing was missing. Apparently. Because deep in his head he had a nagging thought telling him that there was indeed something missing, but he hadn't noticed what.

He went into the bathroom, took a shower, shaved, and got dressed. He picked up his pistol, locked the door, opened the car, got in, slipped the pistol back into the glove compartment, started the engine, and just sat there.

Suddenly he remembered what was missing. He needed to confirm it. He went back into the house, into the bedroom, and reopened the drawer to the nightstand. The burglars had stolen his father's gold watch. They had left the envelope that was on top of it, not realizing there was money in it. And they hadn't tried to steal anything else because they had heard Ingrid arrive.

He felt two contrasting emotions. Anger and relief. Anger because he was attached to that watch; it was one of the few mementos he kept with him. And relief because it was proof that the two men who had entered his house were just a couple of amateurs who clearly had no idea they had broken into the home of a police inspector.

Since he didn't have much to do in his office that morning, he went to the bookshop to restock. Approaching the cash register to pay, he realized all his authors were Swedish: Enquist, Sjöwall-Wahlöö, and Mankell. In unconscious homage to Ingrid? Then he remembered that he needed at least two new shirts. And an extra pair of underpants wouldn't hurt, either. He went off to buy them.

By the time he got to the office, it was almost midday.

"Ahh, Chief, Chief!"

"What's wrong, Cat?"

"I's about to phone you, Chief!"

"What for?"

"Seeing as how I din't see you here, I got a li'l worried. I's afraid you was sick."

"I'm perfectly fine, Cat. Any news?"

"Nuttin', Chief. But Isspector Augello juss came in now sayin' as how he wants me to tell 'im when y'arrived onna premisses."

"You can tell him I'm here."

Mimì appeared, yawning.

"Feeling sleepy? So you slept late and forgot that you were supposed to go to Columba to — "

Mimì raised a hand to stop him, yawned again, noisily, and sat down.

"Since the kid didn't let us get a wink of sleep last night — "

"Mimi, I'm starting to get tired of that excuse. I'm going to phone Beba right now to find out if it's true."

"You'll make a fool of yourself if you do. Beba will only confirm my story. If you would just let me finish speaking — "

"Speak."

"At five o'clock this morning, since I was already wide awake, I headed off for the village of Columba. I guessed they started work early in the morning. The stable was hard to find. You get there by taking the road to Montelusa. A couple of miles on, there's an unmade road on the left, a private driveway that leads to the stable, which is all fenced off. There's a gate with an iron barrier and, next to it, a pole with a button on it. I thought about climbing over the barrier."

"Bad idea."

"And in fact I pushed the button, and a few minutes later a man appeared from a wooden hut and asked me who I was."

"So what'd you do?"

"From the way he spoke and moved, he looked like a caveman. There was no point in talking to him. So I said I was from the police. In a commanding voice. And he let me in right away."

"That wasn't such a good move. We have no authorization to — "

"Come on, the guy didn't ask me anything at all! He didn't even ask me for my name! He was ready to answer all my questions, because he thought I was from Montelusa Central."

46

"But if La Esterman never reported the stolen horse, how — "

"Wait, I'll get to that. We only know half the story of this whole affair. Apparently Lo Duca himself reported the crime to Montelusa Central; it's all rather complicated, as you'll see."

"Why file the report at Montelusa?"

"Because half the stable's property is in our territory, and the other half is in Montelusa's."

"So, what's the story?"

"Wait. First I need to explain to you the layout of the stables. So, just past the barrier, on the left-hand side, are two wooden huts, one rather large, the other much smaller, and a hayloft. The first is the watchman's house; he lives there day and night. The second is used for storing harnesses and everything else needed for the care of horses. On the right-hand side are ten stalls in a row, where they're kept. The last leads to a great big manège."

"And are the horses always there?"

"No, they are put out to pasture in the meadows of La Voscuzza, which belong to Lo Duca."

"But did you find out what actually happened?"

"Did I ever! The troglodyte, what's his name . . . ? Wait a second."

He pulled a sheet of paper out of his jacket pocket and slipped on a pair of glasses. Montalbano froze.

"Mimì!"

It was almost a scream. Augello, stunned, stared at him.

"What is it?"

"You . . . you . . ."

"*O matre santa*, what have I done?"

"You wear glasses now?!"

"Well, yeah."

"Since when?"

"I just picked them up yesterday evening and put them on for the first time today. If they bother you, I can take them off."

"Jesus, you look strange in glasses, Mimì!"

"Strange or not, I needed a pair. And if you want some advice, you ought to have your eyes checked yourself."

"I see perfectly well!"

"That's what you think. But I've noticed that for some time now, when you read, you hold things out at the end of your arm."

"So? What does that mean?"

"It means you're long-sighted. And don't make that face! It's not the end of the world if you have to wear glasses!"

Maybe not the end of the world, but certainly the end of one's prime. Wearing glasses for reading meant surrendering to old age without the least fight.

"So, what's this troglodyte's name?" he asked gruffly.

"Firruzza, Antonio Firruzza. He's the custodian, who for the moment is taking the place of the watchman, whose name is Ippolito Vario."

"And where's the watchman?"

"In the hospital."

"You mean the night the horse was kidnapped, it was Firruzza on guard duty?"

"No, it was Ippolito."

"So Vario's his surname?"

The inspector was distracted. He couldn't take his eyes off the bespectacled Augello.

"No, Vario's his given name."

"I'm not following anything anymore."

"Salvo, if you don't stop continually interrupting me, I'll get lost, too. So, what's it gonna be?"

"OK, OK."

"So, that night, around two o'clock Ippolito was woken up by the sound of the doorbell."

"Does he live alone?"

"Jesus, how annoying! Will you let me speak, or not? Yes, he lives alone."

"I'm sorry. But don't you think a lighter frame would suit you better?"

"Beba likes this one. May I continue?"

"Yes, yes."

"Ippolito gets out of bed thinking it's Lo Duca, back from his travels and with a craving to see his horses. It wouldn't have been the first time. So he gets a torch and goes out to the gate. Bear in mind that it's a very dark night. But as he approaches, he realizes that it's not Lo Duca. He asks the man what he wants, and by way of an answer he points a revolver at him. Ippolito is forced to open the gate with his keys. The man then takes them and whacks Ippolito on the back of the head with the butt of his revolver, knocking him out."

"Which prevented the watchman from seeing anything else. Listen, how strong is the correction on those things?"

Mimì stood up in a huff.

"Where are you going?"

"I'm leaving, and I'm not coming back until you stop fixating on my glasses."

"Come on, sit down. I swear I won't ask anything else about your glasses."

Mimì sat down again.

"Where was I?"

"So the watchman had never seen the man who assaulted him?"

"Never. Anyway, to conclude, Ippolito was found by Firruzza and two other men who take care of the horses, in his house, bound and gagged and with a serious concussion."

"So it could not have been Ippolito who phoned La Esterman to inform her of the theft."

"Obviously."

"Maybe it was Firruzza."

"Firruzza? Impossible."

"So who was it, then?"

"Do you think it's so important? May I continue?"

"Sorry."

"So, Firruzza and the other two men immediately notice two open stalls and realize that two horses have been stolen."

"Two?" said Montalbano, surprised.

"Exactly. Two. Rachele Esterman's horse, and one of Lo Duca's horses that bore a strong resemblance to it."

"Want to bet that when faced with the choice they couldn't make up their minds, and weighing their options, they decided to grab both?"

"That's what I asked Pignataro, and he — "

"Who's Pignataro?"

"One of the two men who look after the horses every day. Matteo Pignataro and Filippo Sirchia. Pignataro maintains that of the five or six people who stole the horses, at least one of them must have known a lot about them. Just think, they took the right harnesses for the two horses, including the saddles. So there wasn't any confusion as to the choice; they took them away knowing exactly what they were doing."

"How did they take them away?"

"In a fully equipped truck. Here and there you can even see some of the tyre tracks."

"Who informed Lo Duca?"

"Pignataro. Who also called the ambulance for Ippolito."

"So it was probably Lo Duca who told Pignataro to inform Esterman."

"You seem stuck on this idea of finding out who informed Esterman. Mind telling me why?"

"Bah, I dunno, really. Anything else?"

"No. Not enough for you?"

"On the contrary. You've done pretty well."

"Thank you, maestro, for the breadth, fullness, and variety of your praises, which deeply move my humble heart."

"Stick it, Mimì."

"So, how should we proceed?"

"With whom?"

"Salvo, this is not the independent republic of Vigàta. Our police department answers to the commissioner's office in Montelusa. Or have you forgotten?"

"So what?"

"Montelusa's got an investigation going. Is it not our duty to inform them exactly how Mrs Esterman's horse was killed here?"

"Mimì, think rationally for a moment. If our colleagues in Montelusa are conducting an investigation, sooner or later they will interrogate Mrs Esterman. Right?"

"Right."

"Mrs Esterman will certainly relate to them, word for word, what she learned from me about her horse. Right?"

"Right."

"At which point our colleagues will race over here to ask us some questions. Which only then will we duly answer. Right?"

"Right. But how come the sum of all these right things is wrong?"

"What do you mean?"

"I mean that our colleagues may ask us why we didn't come to them of our own initiative and tell — "

"*O matre santa!* Mimì, we haven't received a report of this crime, and they haven't said a word to us about the theft of the horses. We're even."

"If you say so."

"To get back to the subject, when you arrived at the stables, how many horses were there in the boxes?"

"Four."

"So, when the thieves got there, there were six."

"Right. But what's the point of counting?"

"I'm not counting. I'm wondering why the thieves didn't steal all the horses while they were at it."

"Maybe they didn't have enough trucks."

"Are you saying that just to be funny?"

"You doubt me? You know what I say to you? That I've talked enough for today. Goodbye."

He stood up.

"But, Mimì, another frame, not necessarily different, since Beba likes this one, but just a wee bit lighter in colour . . ."

Mimì went out cursing, and slammed the door behind him.

What could this business of the two horses mean? No matter which angle he looked at it from, something didn't make sense. For example, Rachele Esterman's horse was stolen and then slaughtered. But then why didn't they just kill it on the spot, instead of dragging it all the way to the beach of Marinella to do it in? And then the other horse, Lo Duca's: did they also steal that one to kill it? And, if so, where? On the beach at Santoli, or somewhere near the stables? Or if they killed one but not the other, what did that mean?

The telephone rang.

"Chief, that'd be Mrs Striomstriommi."

What did Ingrid want?

"On the telephone?"

"Yessir, Chief."

"Put her on."

"Hello, Salvo. Sorry I didn't say goodbye this morning, but I remembered I had an engagement."

"No problem."

"Listen, Rachele phoned me from Fiacca, where she spent last night. She's agreed to race one of Lo Duca's horses, and she's going to spend the afternoon trying to win the animal's confidence, so she's going to stay in Fiacca. She said to me several times how happy she would be if you came with me to see her."

"Would you go there anyway, even if I decided not to come?"

"With a heavy heart, but yes, I would go. I always go when Rachele races."

He weighed his options. Clearly that smart little set would send him into a vertiginous spin, but, on the other hand, it was a unique opportunity to become a little more familiar with the circle of friends, and probably enemies, of Mrs Esterman.

"What time is the race?"

"Tomorrow afternoon at five. If you come, I'll pick you up at your place at three."

Which meant going for a drive straight after eating, on a full stomach.

"Does it take you two hours to drive to Fiacca?"

"No, but we're supposed to get there an hour before the start. It would impolite if we didn't show up till the starting signal."

"All right, then."

"Really? You see? I was right!"

"About what?"

"You did find my friend Rachele attractive."

54

"It's not that; I only accepted so I could spend a few more hours with you."

"You're more phony than . . . than . . ."

"Oh, listen. How should I dress?"

"Naked. You look good naked."

CHAPTER
FIVE

Fazio, who had gone missing all morning, straggled in just before five o'clock.

"You got anything for me?"

"Enough."

"Before you open your mouth, I want you to know that early this morning, Mimì went to Lo Duca's stables and found out some interesting things."

He told him what Augello had discovered. When he had finished, Fazio had a dubious look on his face.

"What's wrong?"

"Sorry, Chief, but wouldn't it be better, at this point, if we got in contact with our colleagues in Montelusa and — "

"And passed the ball to them?"

"Chief, it could be useful to them to know that one of the horses was killed here, in Marinella."

"No."

"Have it your way, then. But could you explain why?"

"If you insist. It's a personal matter. I was really appalled by the stupid ferocity with which they killed that poor animal. I want to see their faces myself."

"But you can tell our colleagues how the horse was killed! With all the details!"

"It's one thing to hear of something, it's another to see it with your own eyes."

"Chief, I'm sorry to be so insistent, but — "

"Are you in cahoots with Augello?"

"Me, in cahoots . . .?!" said Fazio, turning pale.

"Sorry, I'm a bit on edge."

He really was. Because he just remembered he had said yes to Ingrid, and now he no longer felt like going to Fiacca to join the pack of idiots drooling after Rachele.

"Tell me about Prestia."

Fazio was still a touch offended.

"Chief, there are certain things you shouldn't say to me."

"I'll say it again: I'm sorry. OK?"

Fazio pulled a sheet of paper out of his jacket pocket, and the inspector realized that he was going to recite all the personal particulars of Michele Prestia and his associates. Some people collect stamps, Chinese prints, model aeroplanes, and seashells; Fazio collected bureaucratic information on individuals. No doubt when he went home he logged all the information he collected on the people he was investigating onto his computer. And on his days off, he amused himself reviewing it.

"May I?" said Fazio.

"Go ahead."

On other occasions the inspector had threatened him with death if he read his notes out loud. But since he had offended him, he now had to pay. Fazio smiled and started reading. Peace had been made.

"Michele Prestia, known as 'Michilino', born in Vigàta, 23 March 1953, to Giuseppe Prestia and Giovanna née Larosa, and living at Via Abete Meli 32. Married in 1980 to Grazia Stornello, born in Vigàta on 3 September 1960, to Giovanni Stornello and — "

"Couldn't you skip that part?" Montalbano asked timidly, after he had started sweating.

"It's important."

"All right, go on," said the inspector, resigned.

"— and Marianna née Todaro. Michele Prestia and Grazia Stornello had one male child, Balduccio, who passed away in a motorcycle accident at the age of eighteen. After studying bookkeeping at a commercial college, Mr Prestia began working aged twenty as a junior accountant at the firm of Cozzo and Rampello, which presently owns three supermarkets. After ten years he was promoted to accountant. He resigned from this post in 2004, and has remained unemployed to the present day."

He carefully refolded the sheet of paper and slipped it back into his pocket.

"That is all that's officially known," he said.

"And unofficially?"

"Shall I begin with the wedding?"

"Begin wherever you like."

"Michele Prestia met Grazia Stornello at a wedding. From that moment on, he was always after her. They started going out but managed to keep their relationship a secret from everyone. Until one day the

58

girl became pregnant and was forced to tell her parents the whole story. At this point Michilino asked his employers for the leave that was due to him and vanished."

"He didn't want to get married?"

"It was the furthest thing from his mind. But less than a week later, he's back in Vigàta from Palermo, where he had been hiding at a friend's place, and he announces that he's ready to make amends and marry the girl immediately."

"Why did he change his mind?"

"They made him change it."

"Who did?"

"I'll explain. Remember when I said who Grazia Stornello's mother was?"

"Yes, but I don't — "

"Marianna Todaro."

And he cast a knowing glance at the inspector. But Montalbano disappointed him.

"And who's she?"

"What do you mean, who's she? She's one of Balduccio Sinagra's three nieces."

"Wait a second," Montalbano interrupted him. "Are you telling me Balduccio is behind the clandestine horse races?"

"Please, Chief, stop jumping ahead like a kangaroo. I haven't said anything about the clandestine races yet. We were still at the wedding."

"All right, go on."

"So Marianna Todaro goes to see her uncle and tells him about her daughter and so on. At this point Don

Balduccio takes exactly twenty-four hours to locate Michilino in Palermo and has him brought back, to his villa, in the middle of the night."

"Kidnapping."

"You can imagine how frightened Don Balduccio is of being charged with kidnapping!"

"So he threatens him?"

"In his own special way. For two days and two nights he kept him in a totally empty room with nothing to eat or drink. Every three hours somebody came in with a pistol, put a round in the barrel, looked at Michilino, pointed the gun at him, then turned and left without saying a word. On the third day, when Don Balduccio came to see him in person, apologizing for having made him wait — you know what Don Balduccio's like, all smiles and compliments — Michilino got down on his knees, in tears, and asked him for the honour of marrying Grazia. And when the baby was born, they named him Balduccio."

"And how were relations between Balduccio Sinagra and Prestia after that?"

"Well, one year after the wedding, Don Balduccio suggested that he leave his job at Cozzo and Rampello and work for him. But Michilino refused. He told Don Balduccio he was afraid he was unworthy. So Don Balduccio let it drop."

"And after that?"

"Well, after that — and I mean only about four years ago — Michilino developed a gambling habit. Until the day when Messrs Cozzo and Rampello discovered they had a serious cash deficit. Out of respect for Don

Balduccio, they didn't report Prestia to the police, but forced him to resign. But Cozzo and Rampello wanted the stolen money back. They gave him three months."

"Did he ask Don Balduccio for it?"

"Of course. But Don Balduccio told him to fuck himself, saying he wasn't some petty gangster."

"And did Cozzo and Rampello report him?"

"No, they didn't. Because when the three months were up, Michilino came to Messrs Cozzo and Rampello with cash in hand. He paid it all back, down to the last cent."

"Where'd he get it?"

"From Ciccio Bellavia."

Now, there was a name he knew! And how! Ciccio Bellavia had been the rising star of the "*stiddrari*", the new, young Mafia that wanted to stab the old generation of the Sinagras and Cuffaros in the back. But then he betrayed his own comrades and went to work for the Cuffaros, becoming their right-hand man.

So the Mafia was behind the clandestine horse races. It could not have been otherwise.

"So was it Prestia who turned to Bellavia?"

"No, it was the other way around. Bellavia turned up one day, saying he'd heard that Prestia was in trouble and that he was ready to — "

"But Prestia should not have accepted! Taking that money was like announcing he was turning against Balduccio!"

"Didn't I tell you from the start that Michilino Prestia was a nitwit? A cross between a nobody and a nothing? Don Balduccio summed it up when he said he wasn't some petty gangster. Then, to top it off, Prestia had to pay Bellavia back by taking on the responsibility for the illegal races. He couldn't refuse. Which means he's now working against Don Balduccio in business as well."

"I somehow don't see this Prestia ageing gracefully."

"Me neither, Chief. Sorry for asking, but do you still see a connection between the killing of the horse and the illegal races?"

"I don't know what to tell you, Fazio. You don't see any?"

"When you first showed me the dead animal, I was the one, if you recall, who mentioned the clandestine races. But now there doesn't seem to be anything there anymore."

"What do you mean?"

"Chief, every time we form a hypothesis, it gets shot down immediately. Remember you thought that they'd stolen the lady's horse to spite Lo Duca? Then we found out that they also took one of Lo Duca's horses. So what need was there to steal the lady's horse?"

"I agree. But what about the races?"

"Lo Duca, as far as I've been able to find out, has nothing to do with the illegal races."

"You sure about that?"

"Not a hundred per cent sure. I wouldn't bet my life savings on it. But he doesn't really seem like the type to me."

"Never trust appearances. For example, ten years ago, would you have thought Prestia capable of supervising an illegal racing circuit?"

"No."

"So why are you telling me Lo Duca doesn't seem like the type? Let me tell you something else. Lo Duca goes around telling everybody that the Mafia respects him. Or at least they respected him until yesterday. Do you know why he says that? Do you know who his friends are and who protects him?"

"No, Chief, I don't. But I'll try to find out."

"Do you know where these races are held?"

"They change the location practically every time, Chief. I found out that one was held on the grounds behind Villa Panseca."

"Pippo Panseca's house?"

"Yes, sir."

"But, as far as I know, Panseca — "

"Panseca's got nothing to do with it, actually. Perhaps you don't know. When he had to go to Rome for a couple of weeks, the caretaker rented the grounds to Prestia for one night. They paid him so much for it he bought himself a new car. Another time they held it over by Crasto Mountain. Normally, there's one every week."

"Wait a second. Are they always held at night?"

"Of course."

"So how do they see anything?"

"They're very well equipped. You know how when they shoot a film outdoors, they always bring along generators? Well, the ones these guys have got can light everything up like it's daytime."

"But how do they inform their clients of the time and place?"

"The clients who matter most, the high rollers, number only about thirty or forty; the rest are just small fry who, if they come, fine, and if they don't, even better. Too many people in cars create a lot of dangerous confusion."

"But how are they informed?"

"With coded telephone calls."

"And can't we do anything about it?"

"With the means at our disposal?"

The inspector stayed another two hours or so at the station, then drove back to Marinella. Before laying the table on the veranda, he felt like taking a shower. In the dining room he emptied his pockets onto the table, and in so doing he found the piece of paper on which he had written Rachele Esterman's mobile number. He remembered that there was something he wanted to ask her. He could do it the following day, when he saw her in Fiacca. But would it really be possible? God only knew how many people there would be around her. Wasn't it perhaps better to call her now, as it wasn't yet eight-thirty? He decided that this was best.

"Hello? Mrs Esterman?"

"Yes. Who is this?"

"Inspector Montalbano here."

"Oh, no you don't! Don't tell me you've changed your mind!"

"About what?"

"Ingrid told me you were coming here to Fiacca tomorrow."

"I'll be there, signora."

"That makes me so, so happy. Be sure to free yourself for the evening as well. There will be a dinner, and you are one of my guests."

Matre santa! Not a dinner!

"Look, actually, tomorrow evening — "

"Don't make up any silly excuses."

"Will Ingrid also be at the dinner?"

"Can't you take a single step without her?"

"No, it's just that, since she'll be driving me to Fiacca, I was thinking that, for the return — "

"Don't worry, Ingrid will be there. Why did you call me?"

"Why did *I* . . . ?" The prospect of the dinner, the people whose conversation he would have to listen to, the muck that would likely be served and that he would have to swallow, even if it made him vomit, had made him forget that it was he who had called her. "Oh, right, sorry. But I don't want to take up any more of your time. If you could just give me about five minutes tomorrow —"

"Tomorrow there's going to be pandemonium. But I do have a little time right now, before I get ready to go out to eat."

With Guido? A candlelight dinner?

"Listen, signora —"

"Please call me Rachele."

"All right, Rachele. Do you remember when you told me that it was the watchman at the stables who had informed you that your horse — "

"Yes, I remember saying that. But I must have been mistaken."

"Why?"

"Because Chichi — I'm sorry, Lo Duca — told me the poor nightwatchman was at the hospital. On the other hand . . ."

"Go on, Rachele."

"On the other hand I'm almost certain he said he was the watchman. But I'd been asleep, you know, it was very early in the morning and I'd been up very late . . ."

"I understand. Did Lo Duca tell you who he had asked to call you?"

"Lo Duca didn't ask anyone to call me. That would have been ungentlemanly. It was up to him to inform me."

"And did he?"

"Of course! He phoned me from Rome around nine in the morning."

"And did you tell him that someone had already called?"

"Yes."

"Did he make any comment?"

"He said it was probably someone from the stable who had called on his own initiative."

"Have you got another minute?"

"Listen, I'm in the bath and I'm really enjoying it. Hearing your voice so close to my ear right now is . . . Never mind."

She played rough, this Rachele Esterman.

"You told me you phoned the stables in the afternoon — "

"You're not remembering correctly. Someone from the stable called me to tell me the horse hadn't been found yet."

"Did the person identify himself?"

"No."

"Was it the same voice as in the morning?"

"I . . . think so."

"Did you mention this second phone call to Lo Duca?"

"No. Should I have?"

"No, it wasn't necessary. All right, Rachele, I — "

"Wait."

A minute of silence passed. They hadn't been cut off, because Montalbano could hear her breathing. Then she said in a low voice:

"I get it."

"You get what?"

"What you suspect."

"Namely?"

"That the person who called me twice was not from the stables, but was one of the people who stole and killed my horse. Am I right?"

Shrewd, beautiful, and smart.

"You're right."

"Why did they do it?"

"I can't really say at the moment."

There was a pause.

"Oh, listen. Is there any news of Lo Duca's horse?"

"They've lost all trace of it."

"How strange."

"Well, Rachele, that's about all I had — "

"I wanted to tell you something."

"Tell me."

"You . . . I really like you. I like talking to you, being with you."

"Thank you," said Montalbano, a bit confused and not knowing what else to say.

She laughed. And in his mind he saw her naked, in the bathtub, throwing her head back and laughing. A chill ran down his spine.

"I don't think we're going to be able to spend any time together tomorrow, just the two of us . . . Although, maybe — "

She broke off as if she had just thought of something. Montalbano waited a bit, then went *ahem, ahem,* the way they do in English novels.

She resumed speaking.

"At any rate, I've decided to stay another three or four days in Montelusa. I think I already mentioned that to you. I hope we'll have a chance to meet. See you tomorrow, Salvo."

He took a shower and went out on the veranda to eat. Adelina had made a salad of baby octopus big enough for four and some giant langoustines to be dressed only with olive oil, lemon, salt, and black pepper.

He ate and drank, managing only to think of idiocies.

Then he got up and phoned Livia.

"Why didn't you call me yesterday?" was the first thing she said.

How could he tell her he got drunk with Ingrid and it had completely slipped his mind?

68

"There was no way."

"Why not?"

"I was busy."

"With whom?"

Jesus, what a pain in the arse!

"What do you mean, with whom? With my men."

"What were you doing?"

His balls were definitively broken.

"We were having a competition."

"A competition?!"

"Yes, to see who could say the stupidest shit imaginable."

"And you won, of course. You have no rivals in that field!"

And thus began the usual relaxing nightly squabble.

CHAPTER
SIX

After the phone call, he no longer felt like going to bed. He went back out on the veranda and sat down. He needed to distract himself a little, to think about something that had nothing to do with either Livia or the horse case.

The night was calm but quite dark. He could barely see the slightly lighter line of the sea. Out on the water, directly in front of the veranda, was a fishing lamp that in the darkness looked closer than it really was.

At once a taste of lightly fried sole came back to him, between the tongue and palate. He swallowed emptily.

He was ten years old when his uncle took him night-fishing with a lamp for the first and last time, after having pleaded with his wife for an entire evening.

"An' what if the boy falls inna sea?"

"Whas got inna you' head? If 'e falls inna sea, we fish 'im back out. There's two of us, me 'n' Ciccino, c'mon!"

"An' what if 'e's cold?"

"Gimme a sweater. If 'e's cold, I'll make 'im put it on."

"An' what if 'e feels sleepy?"

"He can sleep onna bottom o' the boat."

"An' you, Salvuzzo, you wanna go?"

"Well . . ."

He wanted nothing more, every time his uncle went out to fish. At last his aunt consented, after giving him a thousand warnings.

That night, he remembered, was exactly like this one. Moonless. You could see all the lights along the coast.

After a while, Ciccino, the sixty-year-old sailor who was rowing the boat, said:

"Turn it on."

And his uncle turned on the fishing lamp. A sort of pale blue light, very powerful.

It gave him the impression that the sandy sea bottom had suddenly risen to the surface of the water, completely illuminated. He saw a school of tiny fish which, dazzled by the light, had suddenly frozen, staring at the fishing lamp.

There were transparent jellyfish, a couple of fish that looked like snakes, and some kind of crab crawling along . . .

"You keep leaning out like that, you'll fall in," Ciccino said softly.

Spellbound, he hadn't even realized he was bending so far out of the boat that his face was about to touch the water. His uncle was standing astern, holding the ten-pointed fishgig, its ten-foot shaft tied to his wrist with another ten feet of rope.

"Why," he had asked Ciccino, also softly, so the fish wouldn't flee, "are there two other fishgigs in the boat?"

"One is for fishing by the rocks and the other is for the open sea. One's got firmer points, and the other's sharper."

"And the one that Uncle's got in his hand, what's that?"

"That's a sand fishgig. It's for catching sole."

"Where are they?"

"They're hiding under the sand."

"And how's he see them if they're under the sand?"

"The sole burrow just barely under the sand, so you can still see the little black dots of their eyes. Look, you can see 'em yourself."

He squinted hard, but couldn't see the little black dots.

Then he felt the boat give a jolt and heard the fishgig swoosh powerfully into the water, as his uncle said:

"Got 'im!"

At the end of the fork was a sole as big as his arm, struggling in vain. Two hours later, after he'd caught about ten big soles, his uncle decided to rest.

"Hungry?" Ciccino asked him.

"A little."

"Shall I make you something?"

"Yes."

Boating the oars, the man opened a bag and pulled out a frying pan and a little gas burner, along with a bottle of olive oil, a small bag of flour, and a smaller one of salt. He watched the preparations, mystified. How could anyone eat at that hour of the night? Ciccino, meanwhile, had put the pan on the burner, poured in a bit of oil, floured two soles, and begun to fry them.

"What about you?" his uncle asked.

72

"I'll make mine afterwards. They're too big. Three won't fit in the pan."

While waiting to eat, his uncle told him that the hard thing about fishing with the gig was refraction, and explained what this was. But he didn't understand a thing; all he understood was that the fish looked like it was here, when in fact it was over there.

As soon as the sole began frying, the smell whetted his appetite. He held it over a sheet of newspaper as he ate it, burning his mouth and hands.

In the forty-six years that had passed since that night, he had never experienced the same taste again.

The Milanese Kill on Saturdays was the title of a book of short stories by Scerbanenco that he had read many years ago. And they killed on Saturdays because all the other days they were too busy working.

The Sicilians Don't Kill on Sundays could, on the other hand, have been the title of a book that nobody had ever written.

Because on Sundays the Sicilians go to morning Mass with the whole family, then visit the grandparents, where they stay for lunch; in the afternoon they watch the match on television and, in the evening, again with the whole family, they go out for an ice cream. Where would they find the time to kill anyone on Sundays?

For this reason the inspector decided he would take his shower later than usual, certain he would not be disturbed by a phone call from Catarella.

He got up, opened the French windows. Not a cloud, not a breath of wind.

73

He went into the kitchen, made some coffee, filled two cups, drank one in the kitchen, then took the other one into the bedroom. He took his cigarettes, lighter, and ashtray, set them down on the bedside table, and got back into bed, sitting up with two pillows behind his back.

He drank his coffee, savouring it drop by drop, then lit a cigarette, taking the second drag with double satisfaction. The first satisfaction was the taste of the nicotine on top of that of the caffeine; and the second, the fact that if Livia had been lying beside him, she would have issued the inevitable injunction:

"Either you put out that cigarette, or I'm leaving! How many times have I told you I don't want you smoking in the bedroom?"

And he would have been forced to put it out.

Now, instead, he could smoke the whole damn packet, and blow off the rest of the creation.

"*Wouldn't it be a good idea if you gave a little thought to the investigation?*" Montalbano One asked him.

"*Would you just leave him in peace a moment?*" Montalbano Two intervened, polemicizing with Montalbano One.

"*For a policeman, Sunday is a working day like any other!*"

"*But even God rested on the seventh day!*"

Montalbano pretended not to hear them and kept on smoking. When he'd finished the cigarette, he lay down in the bed and tried closing his eyes again.

74

Little by little, his nostrils began to fill with an ever-so-faint scent, very sweet, a scent that immediately made him think of the naked Rachele in her bathtub . . .

Then he realized that Adelina hadn't changed the pillowcase on which Ingrid had laid her head two nights before, and that his own body heat was releasing the scent of her skin from the cloth.

He tried to put up with this for a few minutes, but failed and had to get out of bed to avoid some perilous uprisings in the south.

A cold shower washed away those wicked thoughts.

"*Why wicked?*" Montalbano One intervened. "*They're perfectly fine and good thoughts!*"

"*At his age?*" Montalbano Two asked maliciously.

When it came time to get dressed, a problem arose.

Adelina didn't come on Sundays, and therefore, as far as eating was concerned, he had no choice but go to Enzo's. But one couldn't get served at Enzo's before twelve-thirty. He wouldn't come out of the trattoria for another hour and a half; in other words, around two.

Would he have time to come back to Marinella and change clothes before Ingrid arrived? Being Swedish, she was sure to show up at three on the dot.

No, the best thing was to get dressed now.

But how? Casual wear would do for the race, but what about the dinner? Could he bring along a small suitcase with a change of clothes? No, that would look silly.

He decided on a grey suit he had worn only twice, for a funeral and a wedding. He got dressed to the nines, putting on a fine shirt and tie, and sparkling shoes. He looked in the mirror and found himself comical.

He took it all off, down to his underpants, and sat down dejectedly on the bed.

Suddenly he thought he'd found a solution: call up Ingrid and say that he'd been shot at, luckily only grazed, but he could no longer . . .

And what if she came running to Marinella? No problem. She would find him in bed with a great big bandage around his head. After all, he had a lifetime's supply of gauze and elastic bandages in the house . . .

"*Come on, try to be serious!*" said Montalbano One. "*These are all excuses! The truth is you don't feel like meeting those people!*"

"*And if he doesn't feel like it, is he still obligated to go, willy nilly? Where is it written that he absolutely has to go to Fiacca?*" countered Montalbano Two.

The upshot was that the inspector turned up at Enzo's at twelve-thirty in his grey suit, but with such a face . . .

"What's wrong, Inspector? Did somebody die?" Enzo asked him, seeing him dressed that way and wearing an expression fit for All Souls' Day.

Montalbano cursed the saints under his breath, but didn't answer the question. He ate without interest. By quarter to three he was back at home. He had just enough time to freshen up, and then Ingrid arrived.

"My, how elegant you are!" she said.

She was in jeans and a blouse.

"Is that what you're wearing to the dinner, too?"

"Of course not! I'm going to change. I've brought everything along."

Why was it so easy for women to take clothes on and off, while for men it was always so complicated?

"Couldn't you go a bit slower?"

"But I'm going very slow."

He'd eaten almost nothing, and yet that little bit leapt up into his gullet every time Ingrid took a curve at seventy-five miles an hour or more.

"Where's the horse race being held?"

"Outside of Fiacca. The Barone Piscopo di San Militello had a genuine racetrack built for the occasion, just behind his villa. It's small but fully equipped."

"And who is the Barone Piscopo?"

"A very gentle, courteous man of about sixty, whose life is devoted to charitable works."

"And he made all his money by being gentle?"

"He inherited his money from his father, a junior partner in a big German steel company, and made some good investments. Speaking of money, have you got any on you?"

Montalbano balked.

"You mean we have to pay to watch the race?"

"No, but you're supposed to place a bet on the winner. It's sort of obligatory."

"Is there a totalizator?"

"Don't be silly! The money from the bets goes to charity."

"And the people who win their bets, what do they get?"

"The woman who wins the race rewards everyone who bet on her with a kiss. But some won't accept."

"Why not?"

"They say it's out of gallantry. But the fact of the matter is that sometimes the winner is downright ugly."

"Do people bet a lot?"

"Not too much."

"How much, more or less?"

"A thousand, two thousand euros. Some bet more, though."

Shit! So what, for Ingrid, would constitute a large bet? A million euros? He felt himself beginning to sweat.

"But I haven't . . ."

"You haven't got that much?"

"In my pocket I've got maybe a hundred euros at the most."

"Have you got your chequebook with you?"

"Yes."

"That's better. A cheque is more elegant."

"All right, but for how much?"

"Make it out for a thousand."

Say what you want about Montalbano, he certainly was not a cheapskate. But to throw away a thousand euros to watch a race in the middle of a sea of arseholes really did not seem like a good thing to do.

When they were about three hundred yards from the Barone Piscopo's villa, they were stopped by a man in brand-spanking-new livery who looked like he'd stepped out of a seventeenth-century painting. The one thing that clashed with the whole picture was that the man had the face of someone who had just got out of Sing-Sing after a thirty-year stint in the cooler.

"You can't go any further in your car," said the convict.

"Why not?"

"There's no more room."

"What are we supposed to do?" asked Ingrid.

"You can walk. Juss leave me the keys an' I'll park it m'self."

"You made us arrive late," Ingrid lamented, as she took a sort of bag from the boot.

"I did?"

"Yes. Always saying, 'Slow down, slow down . . .'"

Cars parked on both sides of the road, cars cluttered the vast patio. In front of the main entrance to the enormous, three-storey villa with a turret on one side stood another man in livery covered with golden squiggles. The butler? He looked to be at least ninety-nine years old and, indeed, was leaning on a sort of shepherd's crook to keep from collapsing.

"Hello, Armando," Ingrid greeted him.

"Hello, signora. Everyone's outside," said Armando in a voice as thin as a spider's web.

"We'll join them straight away. Here, please take this," she said, handing him the bag, "and put it in Mrs Esterman's room."

Armando grabbed the near-weightless bag with one hand, but still it made him list to that side. Montalbano held him up. The man would list if so much as a fly landed on his shoulder.

They crossed a great hall rather like the lobby of some ten-star Victorian hotel, another huge room jam-packed with portraits of ancestors, another room even bigger and jam-packed with suits of armour and featuring three French windows in a row, all open and giving onto a broad, tree-lined lane. So far, aside from the ex-con and the butler, they had not crossed paths with another living soul.

"Where is everybody?"

"They're already there. Hurry."

The lane continued straight for about fifty yards, then split into two, one to the right and the other to the left.

The moment Ingrid took the lane on the left, which was enclosed by very tall hedges, Montalbano, following behind, was met by a noisy barrage of voices, cries, and laughter.

And all at once he found himself on a lawn with small tables and chairs, big umbrellas, and deckchairs. There were even two very long tables with food and drinks and waiters in white jackets. Off to one side was a little wooden cottage with a man standing in its rear window and a queue of people lined up in front of him.

There were at least three hundred men and women crowding the lawn, some sitting, some standing, some speaking or laughing in groups. Beyond the lawn, one could see the so-called racetrack.

People were dressed as if it were Carnival, some in equestrian garb, others in top hats and tails as if attending a reception by the Queen of England, others in jeans and turtlenecks, others in Tyrolean lederhosen and feather caps, others in forest-ranger uniforms (or so they appeared at least to the inspector), one guy in full Arab regalia, and others in shorts and flip-flops. Among the women there were some with hair so big you could have landed a helicopter on it, others in miniskirts up to their armpits, others in maxiskirts so long that anyone who came too close risked tripping up on them and breaking his neck, another in a bowler hat and nineteenth-century riding costume, and a twentyish girl in skin-tight blue-jean short shorts which she could allow herself to wear thanks to the impressive hindquarters with which Mother Nature had endowed her.

When he had finished looking, the inspector noticed that Ingrid was no longer at his side. He felt lost. He had an overwhelming desire to turn tail, walk back up the great lane, through the villa's salons, slip back into Ingrid's car, and —

"Ah, you must be Inspector Montalbano!" said a male voice.

He turned around. The voice belonged to a man of about forty, very thin and very long, wearing a khaki bush jacket, shorts, knee socks, colonial pith helmet, and a pair of binoculars around his neck. He also had a pipe in his mouth. Maybe he thought he was in India at the time of British rule. He held out a soft, sweaty hand that felt to the inspector like wet bread.

"What a pleasure! I am the Marchese Ugo Andrea di Villanella. Are you related to Lieutenant Colombo?"

"The carabinieri lieutenant from Fiacca? No, I'm — "

"Ha ha! I wasn't talking about a lieutenant of the carabinieri, but the Colombo you see on TV, you know, the one in the trench coat whose wife you never see . . ."

Was this guy a cretin or simply trying to make an ass out of the inspector?

"No, actually I'm Inspector Maigret's twin brother," Montalbano replied gruffly.

The marquis looked disappointed.

"I'm sorry, I don't know him."

And he walked away. Decidedly a cretin, and slightly loopy into the bargain.

Another man came forward, dressed as a gardener, in dirty overalls that smelled bad and with a shovel in his hand.

"You seem new here," he said.

"Yes, it's the first time I — "

"Who'd you bet on?"

"Actually, I haven't yet — "

"You want some advice? Bet on Beatrice della Bicocca."

"I don't — "

"Do you know her table of rates?"

"No."

"Let me recite it for you: *Cough up a thousand in euros / and a kiss on the forehead is yours. / A clean five thou without tips / and she'll give you a kiss on the lips. / But find ten grand to shell out; / and you'll find her tongue in your mouth.*"

The man bowed and walked away.

What kind of fucking loony bin had he stumbled into? And wasn't this Beatrice della Bicocca playing unfair?

CHAPTER
SEVEN

"Salvo, come here!"

At last he spotted Ingrid, who was waving her arms as she called him. He headed towards her.

"Inspector Montalbano; the master of the house, the Barone Piscopo di San Militello."

A tall, thin man, the baron was dressed exactly like someone the inspector had seen leading a fox hunt in a movie. Except that the actor in the movie was wearing a red jacket, while the baron's was green.

"Welcome, Inspector," said the baron, extending his hand.

"Thank you," said Montalbano, shaking it.

"Are you enjoying yourself, Inspector?"

"Quite."

"I'm glad."

The baron looked at him, smiling, then clapped his hands loudly. The inspector felt confused. What was he supposed to do? Should he clap his hands, too? Maybe it was a sign these people used on such occasions to express happiness. So he clapped his hands loudly. The baron gave him a puzzled look, and Ingrid started laughing. At that moment a servant in livery handed the baron a coiled horn. So that was why the baron clapped his hands! As Montalbano was blushing for making a fool of himself, the baron brought the horn to his lips and blew. The blast was so loud that it sounded like the "charge" signal for the cavalry. As his head was about three inches away, it left Montalbano's ears ringing.

All fell suddenly silent. The baron passed the horn back to the servant and took the microphone another was handing to him.

"*Mesdames et messieurs!* A moment of attention, please! I hereby inform you that the betting booth will close in ten minutes, after which it will no longer be possible to make any wagers!"

"Please excuse us, Barone," said Ingrid, grabbing Montalbano by the hand and dragging him behind her.

"Where are we going?"

"To place our bets."

"But I don't even know who's racing!"

"Look, there are two favourites. Benedetta di Santo Stefano and Rachele, even though she's not racing her own horse."

"What's this Benedetta like?"

"She's a midget with a moustache. You want to be kissed by her? Now don't be silly; you must bet on Rachele, like me."

"And what is Beatrice della Bicocca like?"

Ingrid stopped dead in her tracks, in disbelief.

"Do you know her?"

"No. I only wanted to know — "

"She's a slut. At this very moment she's probably fucking some stable boy. She always does, before she races."

"Why?"

"Because she says she can feel the horse better afterwards. You know how Formula One drivers feel with their buttocks how well the car is performing? Beatrice can feel how well the horse is performing with her — "

"OK, OK, I get it."

They wrote their cheques at a small, unoccupied table.

"You wait for me here," said Ingrid.

"No, please. I'll go," said Montalbano.

"Look, there's a queue. If I go, they'll let me cut in front of the others."

Not knowing what to do, he approached one of the buffet tables. All that there had been to eat had been dispatched. Nobles, perhaps, but famished as a tribe from Burundi after a drought.

"Would you like something?" a waiter asked him.

"Yes, a J&B, neat."

"There's no more whisky, sir."

He absolutely had to drink something if he was ever going to revive.

"Then a cognac."

"The cognac's finished, too."

"Have you any alcohol left?"

"No, sir. All that's left is orangeade and Coca-Cola."

"An orangeade," he said, sinking into depression before he'd even had a sip.

Ingrid came running up with two slips in her hand, as the baron sounded the second cavalry charge.

"Come, let's go. The baron is calling us all to the racetrack."

And she handed him his slip.

The racetrack was small and rather simple. It consisted of one large, circular track surrounded on either side by a low fence of interwoven branches.

There were also two wooden turrets with nobody in them yet. The starting gates, of which there were six, stood in a row behind the track, still empty. Guests were allowed to stand around the track.

"Let's stay here," said Ingrid. "We're near the finishing post."

They leaned against the fence. A short distance away, there was a white stripe on the ground, which must have been the finish line. Just above it, on the inside of the track, stood one of the turrets, probably reserved for the judges of the race.

Atop the other turret, the Barone Piscopo suddenly appeared, microphone in hand.

"Your attention, please! The line judges, the Conte Emanuele della Tenaglia, Colonel Rolando Romeres, and the Marchese Severino di San Severino, are invited to take their places in the turret!"

Easier said than done. One reached the platform of the turret by way of a small, rather cramped wooden staircase. Considering that the youngest of the three, the marquis, weighed at least twenty stone, that the colonel was about eighty and had the shakes, and that the count had a stiff left leg, the fifteen minutes it took them to get to the top must have been some kind of record.

"Once it took them forty-five minutes to get up there," said Ingrid.

"Is it always the same three?"

"Yes. By tradition."

"Your attention, please! Will the competing ladies please go with their horses to their assigned starting cages!"

"How are the cages assigned?" asked Montalbano.

"They draw lots."

"How come there's no sign of Lo Duca?"

"He's probably with Rachele. The horse she's racing today is one of his."

"Do you know which cage she's got?"

"The first one, the one closest to the inside track."

"And it could not have been otherwise!" commented a man who had overheard their conversation, as he was standing just to the left of Montalbano.

The inspector turned to face him. The man was about fifty and sweaty, and had a head so bald and shiny that it hurt the eyes to look at it.

"What do you mean to say?"

"Exactly what I said. With Guido Costa in charge of it, they have the gall to call it a draw!" said the sweaty man, indignant, before walking away.

"Have you any idea what he was talking about?" he asked Ingrid.

"Of course! The usual nasty gossip! Since Guido is in charge, the man was claiming that the draw was rigged in Rachele's favour."

"So this Guido would be — "

"Yes."

So, in that social circle, it was well known that there was something between the two.

"How many laps do they run?"

"Five."

"Your attention, please! As of this moment, the starter may give the starting signal whenever he deems fit."

Less than a minute passed before a pistol shot rang out.

"And they're off!"

Montalbano was expecting the baron to act as the announcer and commentate the race, but Piscopo di San Militello fell silent, set down the microphone, and picked up a pair of binoculars.

At the end of the first lap, Rachele was in third place.

"Who are the two in the lead?"

"Benedetta and Beatrice."

"Think Rachele will make it?"

"It's hard to say. With a horse she doesn't know . . ."

Then they heard a great roar, and on the far side of the track there was a commotion and a lot of people running.

"Beatrice has fallen," said Ingrid. Then she added, maliciously, "Maybe she didn't put herself in the right condition to feel the horse properly."

"*Mesdames et messieurs!* I inform you that rider Beatrice della Bicocca has fallen from her horse, but luckily with no untoward consequences whatsoever."

After the second lap, Benedetta was still in the lead, though followed closely by a rider the inspector didn't recognize.

"Who's she?" he asked.

"Veronica del Bosco, who shouldn't be any problem for Rachele."

"But why hasn't Rachele taken advantage of the fall?"

"No idea."

As they began the final lap, Rachele moved up into second place. For about fifty yards she engaged in a tight, rousing head-to-head dash with Benedetta, as the crowd seemed to go completely mad with shouting. Even Montalbano found himself yelling:

"Come on, Rachele! Come on!"

Then, about thirty yards from the finish line, Benedetta's horse seemed to grow ten extra legs, and there wasn't much Rachele could do about it.

"Too bad!" said Ingrid. "If she'd had her own horse, she would surely have won. Are you sorry?"

"Well, a little."

"Mostly because you won't be kissed by Rachele, right?"

"So what do we do now?"

"Now the baron is going to read the results."

"What results? We already know who won."

"Just wait. They're interesting."

Montalbano torched a cigarette. Three or four people who were standing near him stepped away, staring at him with annoyance.

"*Mesdames et messieurs!*" the baron called out from his turret. "It is my pleasure to announce to you that the sum total of the bets amounts to over six hundred thousand euros! I am truly grateful to all of you."

Since there were about three hundred people present, and most were either blue bloods or businessmen or landowners, you couldn't exactly say they had opened their wallets.

"The rider who received the highest number of bets was Signora Rachele Esterman!"

The crowd applauded. Rachele had lost the race, but raised the most money.

"I ask our distinguished guests please not to linger on the lawn, where we shall need to set up the tables for dinner, but to gather in the salons inside the villa."

When Montalbano and Ingrid turned their backs on the track, the last thing they saw were two servants who, having picked up Colonel Romeres, were lowering him from the turret.

"I'm going to go and change," said Ingrid, slipping away. "See you in about an hour, in the salon of the ancestors."

Montalbano went into the salon, found a mysteriously unoccupied armchair, and sat down. He had to get through an hour without thinking about what he had realized as he was watching the race, which had put him on edge. He had noticed that he couldn't see very well. There was no denying it. Each time the horses were running on the far side of the track from where he stood, he could no longer make out the different colours of the riders' silks. Everything became muddled, the outlines blurred. If not for Ingrid he would not even have realized that it was Beatrice della Bicocca who had fallen.

"Well, what's so unusual about that?" asked Montalbano One. "It's old age. Mimì Augello was right."

"That's nonsense!" Montalbano Two rebelled. "Mimì Augello says you hold things at arm's length in order to read. That's long-sightedness, which is typical of ageing. Whereas what we have here is short-sightedness, which has nothing to do with age!"

"Then what's it got to do with?"

"It could be fatigue, a temporary loss of — "

"Whatever the case, it wouldn't be a bad idea to go have — "

The discussion was interrupted by a man who planted himself directly in front of the armchair.

"Inspector Montalbano! Rachele had told me you were here, but I couldn't find you."

It was Lo Duca. About fifty, tall, most distinguished, most tanned from sunlamps, most glistening smile, salt-and-pepper hair groomed to perfection. One could only use superlatives to describe him. Montalbano stood up, and they shook hands. He was most fragrant as well.

"Why don't we go outside?" Lo Duca suggested. "It's stifling in here."

"But the baron said . . ."

"Never mind the baron. Come with me."

They passed back through the salon of armour, went out through one of the French windows, but instead of taking the broad lane, Lo Duca immediately turned left. On this side there was a very well-tended garden with three gazebos. Two had people in them, but the third was free. It was starting to get dark, but one of the gazebos had its light on.

"You want me to turn on the light?" asked Lo Duca. "Take my word for it, however, it's better if we don't. We'd be eaten alive by mosquitoes. Which will happen anyway during dinner."

There were two comfortable wicker easy chairs and a little table with a vase of flowers and an ashtray on it. Lo Duca took out a packet of cigarettes and held it out to the inspector.

"Thanks, but I prefer my own."

They lit their cigarettes.

"Excuse me for getting straight to the point," said Lo Duca. "Perhaps you don't feel like talking about work at the moment, but — "

"Not at all, go right ahead."

"Thank you," Lo Duca began. "Rachele told me she went to the Vigàta police to report the disappearance of her horse, but then didn't file the report after you told her it had been killed."

"Right."

"Rachele was probably too upset when you told her the horse had been destroyed in a particularly brutal manner; in fact she was unable to be more specific — "

"Right."

"But how did you find out?"

"It was pure chance. The horse came and died right outside my window."

"But is it true that a bit later somebody came and removed the carcass?"

"Right."

"Do you have any idea why?"

"No. Do you?"

"Perhaps, yes."

"Tell me, if you would."

"Of course I'll tell you. If and when the body of Rudy, my horse, is found, it probably will have been killed in the same manner. This is a vendetta, Inspector."

"And did you present this hypothesis of yours to my colleagues in Montelusa?"

"No. Just as you, from what I've heard, haven't yet told your colleagues in Montelusa that you found Rachele's horse."

Touché. Lo Duca certainly knew how to fence.

The inspector had to proceed carefully.

"A vendetta, you say?"

"Yes."

"Could you be a little more precise?"

"Yes. Three years ago I had a heated argument with one of the men who used to tend my horses, and in a fit of anger, I struck him in the head with an iron bar. I didn't think I had hurt him too badly, but it left him disabled. Naturally I took care of all the medical expenses, but I also give him a monthly stipend equal to the pay he used to receive."

"But, if that's the way it is, why would this man want — "

"Well, it's been three months since his wife has had any news of him. He was no longer right in the head. One day he left muttering threats against me and hasn't

94

been seen since. There are rumours he has taken up with criminals."

"Mafiosi?"

"No, just common criminals."

"But why didn't this man limit himself to stealing and killing your horse? Why did he also take Mrs Esterman's horse?"

"I don't think he knew the horse wasn't mine when he was stealing it. He probably realized it afterwards."

"And you didn't mention this to my colleagues in Montelusa, either?"

"No. And I don't think I will."

"Why not?"

"Because I feel it would be hounding an unlucky wretch whose mental infirmity I am responsible for."

"So why did you bring it up with me?"

"Because I've been told that when you want to get to the bottom of something, you do."

"Well, since I'm someone who gets to the bottom of things, as you say, could you tell me this person's name?"

"Gerlando Gurreri. But could I have your word that you will not mention this name to anyone?"

"No need to worry. However, you've given me the motive, but you haven't told me why they removed the horse's carcass."

"As I said, I believe that when Gurreri stole the two horses, he thought they were both mine. Then an accomplice must have pointed out that one of them belonged to Rachele. So they killed it and then removed the carcass, leaving me to stew in my doubts."

95

"I don't understand."

"Inspector, how can you be so sure that the horse you found dead on the beach was Rachele's and not mine? When they took away the remains, they made identification impossible. So, by leaving me in a state of uncertainty, they are making me suffer even more. Because I was very attached to my Rudy."

The argument made a certain sense.

"Tell me something, Mr Lo Duca. Who was it that informed Mrs Esterman that her horse had been stolen?"

"I thought I did. But apparently someone beat me to it."

"Who?"

"I don't know, maybe one of the two who tend the horses. Rachele, moreover, had given the watchman the telephone numbers where she could be reached. The watchman kept that piece of paper pinned inside the front door of his house. It's still there, in fact. Is that of any importance?"

"Yes, it's very important."

"How so?"

"You see, Mr Lo Duca, if nobody from the stable called Mrs Esterman, it means that it was Gerlando Gurreri."

"And why would he do it?"

"Maybe because he thought that you would wait as long as possible before informing Mrs Esterman of the theft of her horse, in the hopes of recovering it quickly, perhaps by paying a big ransom."

"In other words, to make me lose face and embarrass me in everyone's eyes?"

"It's a possibility, don't you think? But if you tell me that Gurreri, who you say is a bit off his rocker, is not in any condition to reason so subtly, then my hypothesis crumbles."

Lo Duca paused to think about this.

"Well," he said after a brief moment, "I suppose it's possible that it wasn't Gerlando who cooked up the scheme of the telephone call, but one of the crooks he's fallen in with."

"That, too, is quite likely."

"Salvo? Where are you?"

Ingrid was calling him.

CHAPTER
EIGHT

Saverio Lo Duca stood up. Montalbano likewise.

"I'm sorry to have troubled you for so long, but, as I am sure you realize, I didn't want to miss this precious opportunity."

"Salvo? Where are you?" Ingrid called again.

"Oh, not at all!" said the inspector. "In fact, I'm sincerely grateful for what you've been so kind as to reveal to me."

Lo Duca gave a hint of a bow, Montalbano as well.

Not even in the nineteenth century could a more polished and elegant dialogue have taken place, say, between the Visconte di Castelfrombone (a descendant of de Bouillon) and the Duca di Lomantò, immortalized by the Quartetto Cetra.

They turned the corner. Ingrid, looking quite chic, was standing in front of one of the French windows, looking around.

"Here I am," said the inspector, waving an arm.

"I'm sorry to abandon you, but I need to meet . . ." said Lo Duca, picking up his pace and walking away without ever saying who it was he was supposed to meet.

At that moment, the peal of a powerful gong rang out. Perhaps they had put a microphone in front of it. Whatever the case, it sounded like the start of an earthquake. And an earthquake it was.

From the interior of the villa, a disorderly chorus thundered:

"The gong! The gong!"

Everything that followed was exactly like an avalanche or a river bursting its banks.

Pushing and shoving, tripping and colliding, a surge of shouting women and men crashed through the three French windows and poured out onto the broad lane. In an instant, Ingrid receded from sight, caught in the middle and irresistibly swept downstream. Turning around towards him, she opened her mouth and said something, but the words were incomprehensible. It was like the ending of a tragic film. Bewildered, Montalbano had the impression that a terrible blaze had broken out inside the villa, but the cheerful faces of everyone in the wild stampede told him that he was mistaken. Getting out of the way to avoid being bowled over, he waited for the flood to pass. The gong had announced that the dinner was ready. Why was it that these aristos, entrepreneurs, and businessmen were always so hungry? They had already polished off two long tablefuls of antipasti, and still they acted as though they hadn't eaten for a week.

When the flood subsided into a little rivulet of three or four stragglers running like hundred-metre sprinters, Montalbano ventured to step back onto the broad lane. Good luck finding Ingrid! But what if, instead of going to eat, he were to ask the ex-con for the car keys, slip inside, and take a two-hour nap? He thought this seemed like an excellent idea.

"Inspector Montalbano!" he heard a woman's voice call.

He turned towards the salon and saw Rachele Esterman coming out. At her side was a fiftyish man in a dark grey suit, the same height as her, with very little hair and the face of a spy.

By "the face of a spy" the inspector meant an utterly anonymous face, one of those you could have before you for an entire day but still not remember the next. Faces like James Bond's are not spy faces, because once you've seen them you never forget them, and thus the danger of recognition by the enemy is all the greater.

"Guido Costa, Inspector Montalbano," said Rachele.

The inspector had to make a considerable effort to stop looking at Rachele and turn his gaze towards Costa. The moment he saw her, he was spellbound. She was wearing a sort of black sack held up by her very slender shoulders and hanging down to her knees. Her legs were longer and more beautiful than Ingrid's. Hair loose and brushing her shoulders, a ring of precious stones around her neck. In her hand she held a shawl.

"Shall we go?" said Guido Costa.

He had the voice of a dubber of porn flicks, one of those warm, deep voices that are used to whisper filthy things into women's ears. Perhaps the insignificant Guido had some hidden qualities.

"Who knows if we'll ever find a place to sit down," said Montalbano.

100

"Not to worry," said Rachele. "I've reserved a table for four. But it's going to be a challenge to find Ingrid."

It wasn't. Ingrid was waiting for them, standing, at the reserved table.

"I ran into Giogiò!" Ingrid said cheerfully.

"Ah, Giogiò!" said Rachele with a little smile.

Montalbano intercepted a complicit look between the two women and understood everything. Giogiò must have been an old flame of Ingrid's. And whoever said that reheated soup isn't good might well be mistaken in this case. The inspector shuddered in terror at the thought that Ingrid might decide to spend the night with the rediscovered Giogiò, leaving him to sleep in the car until morning.

"Would you mind if I went and sat at Giogiò's table?" Ingrid asked the inspector.

"Not at all."

"You're an angel."

She leaned down and kissed him on the forehead.

"On the other hand . . ."

"Don't worry. I'll come and get you after dinner, and we'll drive back to Vigàta together."

The head waiter, who had witnessed the whole scene, came forward and removed Ingrid's table settings.

"Is the placement all right, Mrs Esterman?"

"Yes, Matteo, thank you."

And as the head waiter was walking away, she explained to Montalbano:

"I asked Matteo to reserve us a table at the edge of the lighted area. It's a bit dark for eating, but to make

101

up for that, we'll be spared the mosquitoes, at least up to a point."

All across the lawn were dozens and dozens of tables of various sizes, with four to ten places, under the violent glare of several floodlights mounted on four iron towers. Surely swarms of millions and millions of mosquitoes from Fiacca and neighbouring towns were cheerfully converging towards this immense light source.

"Guido, if you would be so kind, I forgot my cigarettes in my room."

Without a word, Guido got up and headed towards the villa.

"Ingrid told me you bet on me. Thanks. I owe you a kiss."

"You ran a good race."

"If I'd had my poor Super, I would surely have won. Speaking of which, I've lost track of Chichi — I'm sorry, I mean Lo Duca. I wanted to introduce you to him."

"We've already met, and we even talked."

"Oh, really? Did he tell you his theory about the two stolen horses and why they killed mine?"

"You mean the vendetta hypothesis?"

"Yes. Do you think it's possible?"

"Why not?"

"Chichi has been a real gentleman, you know. He wanted at all costs to reimburse me for the loss of Super."

"You refused?"

"Of course. What fault is it of his? Oh, indirectly, I suppose . . . But, the poor man . . . He's been so mortified by all this . . . I even kidded him a little about it."

"About what?"

"Well, you see, he likes to brag that he has the respect of everyone in Sicily, and he goes around saying that no one would ever dare do anything to harm him. Whereas — "

A waiter appeared with three plates, set them down at each place, and left.

In them was a thin, yellowish soup with greeny little streaks, the smell of which was a cross between beer gone sour and turpentine.

"Shall we wait for Guido?" Montalbano asked. Not out of politeness, but merely to stall, so he could summon the courage needed to put that first spoonful in his mouth.

"Of course not. It'll get cold."

Montalbano filled the spoon, brought it to his lips, closed his eyes, and swallowed. He was hoping that it would have at least the same taste/non-taste as soup-kitchen soups, but it turned out to be worse. It burned the throat. Maybe they'd seasoned it with hydrochloric acid. At the second spoonful, which was half air, he opened his eyes and realized that, in a flash, Rachele had eaten all of hers, since the dish in front of her was completely empty.

"If you don't like it, give it to me," said Rachele.

But how could she possibly like that disgusting swill? He passed her his dish.

She took it, leaned down slightly to one side, emptied it out on the grass, and handed it back to him.

"This is one advantage of a poorly lit table."

Guido returned with the cigarettes.

"Thank you. Eat your soup, dear, before it gets cold. It's delicious. Don't you think, Inspector?"

Surely the woman must have a sadistic streak. Obediently, Guido Costa ate all his soup in silence.

"It was good, wasn't it, dear?" Rachele asked.

And under the table, her knee knocked twice against Montalbano's in understanding.

"It wasn't bad," the poor bastard replied, voice suddenly cracking.

The hydrochloric acid must have burnt his vocal cords.

Then, for a moment, a cloud seemed to have passed in front of the floodlights.

The inspector looked up. It was a cloud all right — of mosquitoes. A minute later, amid the voices and laughter one began to hear a chorus of whacks. Men and women were slapping themselves, smacking themselves on the neck, forehead, and ears.

"So where has my shawl ended up?" asked Rachele, looking under the table.

Montalbano and Guido also bent down to look. They didn't find it.

"I must have dropped it on the way here. I'm going to go and get another; I don't want to be eaten up by mosquitoes."

"I'll go," said Guido.

"You're a saint. You know where it is? Probably in the large suitcase. Or else in one of the drawers of the cupboard."

So there was no longer any doubt that they slept together. They were too intimate for this not to be the case. But then why did Rachele treat him this way? Did she like having him as her servant?

As soon as Guido left, Rachele said:

"Excuse me."

She stood up. And Montalbano was flummoxed, because Rachele then blithely picked up the shawl, which she had been sitting on, wrapped it around her shoulders, smiled at the inspector, and said:

"I have no desire to keep eating this slop."

She took barely two steps before disappearing into the darkness just behind the table. Should he follow her? But she hadn't said he should. Then he saw the flame of a cigarette lighter in the darkness.

Rachele had lit up a cigarette and was smoking, standing a few yards away. Maybe she felt suddenly in a bad mood and wanted to be alone.

The waiter arrived, again with three plates. This time it was fried mullet.

The unmistakable stink of fish that had been dead for a week wafted into the terrified inspector's nostrils.

"Salvo, please come here."

He didn't so much obey Rachele's call as genuinely flee the mullet on his plate. Anything was better than eating it.

He drew near to her, guided by the little red dot of her cigarette.

"Stay with me."

He enjoyed watching her lips appear and then disappear with each drag she took.

When she had finished, she threw the butt onto the ground and crushed it with her shoe.

"Let's go," she said.

Montalbano turned around to go back to their table, then heard her laugh.

"Where are you going? I want to go say goodbye to Moonbeam. They'll be coming to pick him up early tomorrow morning."

"I'm sorry, but what about Guido?"

"He'll wait. What did they serve as the main course?"

"Mullet caught at least eight days ago."

"Guido won't have the nerve not to eat it."

She took his hand.

"Come. You don't know your way around here. I'll be your guide."

Montalbano's hand felt comforted to be cuddled in that soft, warm nest.

"Where are the horses?"

"On the left side of the racing fence."

There were in a sort of thicket, in complete darkness. He couldn't find his way, and this bothered him. He risked knocking his head against a tree. But the situation immediately improved when Rachele moved Montalbano's hand onto her hip and then rested her own on top, so that they continued walking in each other's embrace.

"Is that better?"

"Yes."

Of course it was better. Now Montalbano's hand was doubly comforted: by the heat of the woman's body, and by the heat of the hand she kept on top of his. All at once the thicket came to an end, and the inspector saw before him a large, grassy clearing, at the far end of which a dim light glowed.

"See that light up ahead? That's where the stalls are."

Now that he could see better, Montalbano began to retract his hand, but she was ready and squeezed it harder.

"Leave it like that. Do you mind?"

"N . . . no."

He heard her giggle. Montalbano was walking with his head down, looking at the ground, afraid to misstep or bump into something.

"I don't understand why the baron had this gate put here. It makes no sense. I've been coming here for years, and it's always the same," Rachele said after a while.

Montalbano looked up. He caught a glimpse of a cast-iron gate that was open.

There was nothing around it, neither a wall nor a fence. It was a perfectly useless gate.

"I simply cannot understand what its purpose is," Rachele repeated.

Without knowing why, the inspector felt overwhelmed by a powerful sense of uneasiness. Like when you find yourself in a place where you know you've never been, and yet you feel like you've been there before.

When they arrived in front of the stalls, Rachele let go of Montalbano's hand and slipped out of his embrace. Out of one of the stalls popped the head of a horse that had somehow sensed her presence. Rachele went up to it, brought her mouth to its ear, and started talking to it in a soft voice. She stroked its forehead for a long while, left off, then turned towards Montalbano, walked up to him, embraced him, and kissed him — a long, deep kiss, with her entire body pressed up against his. To the inspector it seemed as if the ambient temperature had spiked by about twenty degrees. Then she stepped back.

"That's not, however, the kiss I would have given you if I had won."

Montalbano said nothing, still stunned. She took him by the hand again and led him away.

"Where are we going now?"

"I want to give Moonbeam something to eat."

She stopped in front of a small hayloft. The door was locked, but a brisk tug was enough to open it. The scent of hay was so strong it was stifling. Rachele went inside, and the inspector followed. As soon as they were inside, she closed the door behind them.

"Where's the light?"

"Never mind."

"But you can't see a thing this way."

"I can," said Rachele.

And at once he felt her, naked, in his arms. She had undressed in the twinkling of an eye.

The scent of her skin was overpowering. Hanging from Montalbano's neck, her mouth glued to his, she let herself fall backwards onto the hay, pulling him down on top of her. Montalbano was so astounded that he felt like a mannequin.

"Put your arms around me," she ordered, in a voice suddenly different.

Montalbano embraced her. Then, after a brief spell, she turned around until she was facing away from him.

"Mount me," said the coarse voice.

He turned and looked at the woman.

She was no longer a woman, but sort of a horse. She had got down on all fours . . .

The dream!

That was what had made him feel so uneasy! The absurd gate, the horse-woman . . . He froze for a moment, let go of the woman . . .

"What's got into you? Put your arms around me!" Rachele repeated.

"C'mon, mount me," she repeated.

He mounted and she took off at a gallop like a rocket . . .

Later he felt her move and then get up, and all at once a yellowish light lit up the scene. Rachele, still naked, was standing beside the door by the light switch and looking at him. Without warning she started laughing in her way, throwing her head back.

"What's wrong?"

"You're funny. You're so touching."

She went up to him, knelt down, and hugged him. Montalbano started frantically putting his clothes back on.

But they lost another ten minutes helping each other remove the blades of hay that had lodged themselves in every place they could.

They retraced their steps without a word, and walking a bit apart from each other.

Then, just as he had feared, Montalbano ran into a tree. But this time Rachele did not come to his aid by taking his hand. She said only:

"Did you hurt yourself?"

"No."

But when they were still in the dark part of the great lawn where the tables were, Rachele suddenly put her arms around him and whispered in his ear:

"I really enjoyed you."

Deep inside, Montalbano felt a kind of shame. He also felt slightly offended.

I really enjoyed you! What kind of fucking statement was that? What did it mean? That the lady was satisfied with the performance? Pleased with the product? Try Montalbano's cassata; you'll taste paradise! Montalbano's ice cream has no equal! Montalbano's cream horns are the best! Try them, you'll like them!

He felt enraged. Because, while Rachele might have enjoyed the encounter, it was still stuck in his throat. What had taken place between the two of them, anyway? A pure and simple coupling. Like two horses in a barn. And he, after a certain point, had been unable, or had not known how, to restrain himself.

110

How true it was that one needed to slip only once, to slip every time thereafter!

Why had he done it?

It was a pointless question, in that he knew very well why: the fear — by now ever-present even when not visible — of the years passing by, flying by. And his having been first with that twenty-year-old girl, whose name he did not even want to remember, and now with Rachele, were both ridiculous, miserable, pitiable attempts to stop time. To stop it, at least, for those few seconds in which only the body was alive, while the mind, for its part, was lost in some great, timeless nothingness.

When they returned to their table, the dinner was over. A few tables had already been cleared by the waiters. A dreary atmosphere hung over it all, and a few of the floodlights had been turned off. A handful of people remained, still willing to be eaten alive by mosquitoes.

Ingrid was waiting for them at Guido's place.

"Guido has gone back to Fiacca," she said to Rachele. "He was a bit miffed. He said he'll call you later."

"All right," Rachele said indifferently.

"Where'd you two go?"

"Salvo came with me to say goodbye to Moonbeam."

Ingrid gave a hint of a smile at the sound of that "Salvo".

"I'm going to smoke this cigarette and then go beddy-bye," said Rachele.

Montalbano also lit up. They smoked in silence. Then Rachele stood up and exchanged kisses with Ingrid.

"I'll come to Montelusa late in the morning."

"Whenever you like."

Then she put her arms around Montalbano and rested her lips lightly on his.

"I'll call you tomorrow."

As soon as Rachele left, Ingrid leaned forward, reached out with her hand, and started feeling around in the inspector's hair.

"You're full of straw."

"Shall we go?"

"Let's."

CHAPTER
NINE

They got up. In the salons they encountered barely ten people.

A few of them lay sprawled out in armchairs, half asleep. Since it wasn't very late, the soup and putrid mullets must have had an effect somewhere between food poisoning and heaviness in the stomach. The courtyard had already nearly been emptied of cars.

They walked the three hundred yards of road until they saw Ingrid's car, now alone, parked under an almond tree. But there was no sign of the ex-con in the vicinity. He had thought, however, to leave the keys in the door.

Since it was night and there was little traffic, Ingrid felt entitled to drive at an average speed of about ninety. What's more, when she passed a heavy goods vehicle on a curve with another car fast approaching head-on, Montalbano, in that instant, was able to read his own obituary in the newspaper. This time, however, he didn't want to give her the satisfaction of telling her to slow down.

Ingrid wasn't talking. She was driving alertly, tongue pressed between her lips, but it was clear she was not in her usual mood. She didn't open her mouth until Marinella came into view.

"Did Rachele get what she wanted?" she began brutally.

"Thanks to your help."

"What do you mean?"

"That you and Rachele had agreed on a plan, perhaps when you were changing for dinner. She probably told you she would like — how shall I put it? — to taste me. And you cleared out, inventing some Giogiò who never existed. Am I right?"

"Yeah, yeah, you're right."

"So then what's wrong?"

"I'm having a belated attack of jealousy, OK?"

"No, it's not OK. It's illogical."

"I'll leave the logic to you. I have a different way of thinking."

"Namely?"

"Salvo, the fact is that with me you play the saint, and with other women — "

"But it was you who acted as my sponsor for Rachele, I am sure of it!"

"Your sponsor?!"

"Yes, ma'am! '*You know, Rachele, Montalbano's cassata is the best there is! Try and see for yourself!*'"

"What the hell are you talking about?"

They pulled up at his house. Montalbano got out of the car without saying goodbye. Ingrid, too, got out, and planted herself in front of him.

"Are you mad at me?" she asked.

"At you, at me, at Rachele, at all of creation!"

114

"Just listen for a second. Let's be frank, Salvo. It's true that Rachele asked me if she could give it a go, and I cleared out. But it's equally true that, when you were alone with her, she hardly pointed a gun at you and forced you to do what she wanted. She asked you, in her way, and you consented. You could have said no, and that would have been the end of that. You have no right to be mad at me or Rachele. Only at yourself."

"OK, but — "

"Let me finish. I also understand what you meant by your cassata. What, did you want feeling? Did you want a declaration of love? Did you want Rachele to whisper passionately to you: 'I love you, Salvo. You're the only person in the world I love'? Did you want deep feelings for an excuse, so you could have your quickie and feel less guilty? Rachele, quite honestly, offered you — wait, how shall I put it? — ah, yes: she offered you a deal. And you accepted."

"Yes, but — "

"And you want to know something else? You disappointed me a little."

"Why?"

"I really thought you would be able to handle Rachele. And now that's enough. I apologize for the rant. Good night."

"I apologize, too."

The inspector waited for Ingrid to leave, waved goodbye, then turned, opened the door, flicked on the light, went inside, and froze.

The burglars had turned the house upside down.

After spending half an hour trying to put everything back in its proper place, he lost heart. Without Adelina's help, he would never manage. He might as well leave things just as they were. It was almost one o'clock in the morning, but sleep was the last thing on his mind. The burglars had forced open the French windows on the veranda, and it must not have even required much effort, because when Ingrid had come by to pick him up, he had forgotten to lock the dead bolt. A thrust of the shoulder had sufficed to open it.

He went into the utilities cupboard where the housekeeper kept the things she needed, and he noticed that they had carefully searched even there. The tool drawer had been opened, its contents scattered across the floor. At last he found the hammer, screwdriver, and three or four small screws. But the moment he tried to fix the lock on the French windows, he realized he really did need glasses.

But how could he have never noticed before that his vision was faulty? His mood, already dark because of Rachele and the lovely surprise he had come home to, became even darker, black as ink. All at once he remembered that in the drawer of the nightstand was a pair of glasses of his father's that had been sent to him together with the watch.

He went into the bedroom and opened the drawer. The envelope with the money was still in its place, as was the glasses case.

But he also found something he hadn't expected to find. The watch had been put back.

116

He put on the glasses and his vision immediately improved. He went back into the dining room and started fixing the lock.

The burglars — who, it was clear, should no longer be called that — hadn't stolen anything. Indeed, they had even given back what they had taken during their first visit.

And this was a clear, indeed unscrambled, message: *Dear Montalbano, We did not break into your house to rob you, but to look for something.*

Had they found it, after a search more thorough than anything he'd ever seen the police do? And what could it be?

A letter? But at home he didn't have any correspondence that might matter to anyone.

A document? Something written that had something to do with an investigation? But he very rarely brought any paperwork home with him and, anyway, he always took it back to the station the next day.

Whatever the case, the conclusion was that if they hadn't found it, then surely they would be back again for another go-round even more devastating than the first.

His little repair job on the French windows seemed to him to have come out well. He opened and closed it twice, and the spring lock seemed to work.

"*See? When you retire, you can devote yourself to little household chores like this,*" said Montalbano One.

He pretended not to have heard. The night air had brought with it the scent of the sea and, as a result,

117

whetted his appetite. During the preceding day he'd eaten hardly anything at lunchtime, and in the evening only two spoonfuls of the hydrochloric-acid soup. He opened the refrigerator: green olives, black passuluna olives, caciocavallo cheese, anchovies. The bread was a bit hard but still edible. There was no lack of wine. He put together a nice platter of what he had and took it out onto the veranda.

Clearly the burglars — *for the moment we'll keep calling them that,* he said to himself — must have taken a great deal of time to be able to search the house as they had done. Did they know he was out of town and wouldn't be back until late at night? And if they did, that meant someone had informed them. But who knew he was going to Fiacca that evening? Only Ingrid and Rachele.

Wait a second, Montalbano, don't start running with this, or you're liable to trip and fall onto a pile of crap.

The simplest explanation was that they were keeping an eye on him. And the moment they saw him leave, they had forced open the French windows in broad daylight. Besides, who would have been on the beach at that hour? Then they went inside and had the rest of the afternoon to work in peace.

Hadn't they done the same thing the first time? They had waited for him to go out to buy whisky, and then gone inside. Yes, they were keeping an eye on him. Spying on him.

And it was possible that even now, as he was eating his olives and bread, they were watching him. Shit, what a pain in the arse!

He felt deeply disturbed to know that his every movement was being observed by people unknown. He hoped they had found what they were looking for, so they could stop breaking his balls.

Having finished eating, he got up, took the plate, cutlery, bottle, and glass into the kitchen, locked the French windows, congratulating himself on his repair job, and went to take a shower. As he was washing himself, a few blades of straw fell from his head to his feet, before they were swallowed up by the small whirlpool around the drain.

He woke up to the screams of Adelina, who came running into his bedroom, scared out of her wits.

"*O matre di dio! O madunnuzza santa!* Wha' happen?"

"Burglars, Adeli."

"Burglars in you' house, sir?"

"So it seems."

"Wha'd they steal?"

"Nothing. Actually, do me a favour. As you're putting things back in order, check and see if anything's missing."

"OK. You wanna some coffee?"

"Of course."

He drank it in bed. And, still in bed, he smoked his first cigarette.

Then he went into the bathroom, got dressed, and returned to the kitchen for a second cup.

"Know what, Adeli? Yesterday evening, in Fiacca, I had some soup and, I'm sorry to say, I've never tasted anything quite like it."

"Really, signore?" said Adelina, displeased.

"Really. I had them give me the recipe. Soon as I can find it, I'll read it for you."

"Signore, I dunno if I gotta nuffa time a tidy uppa you' whole house."

"That's OK. Do as much as you can. You can finish tomorrow."

"Ah, Chief, Chief! How'd ye spenn your Sunday?"

"I went to see some friends in Fiacca. Who's here?"

"Fazio's onna premisses. Should I oughta call 'im?"

"No, I'll go and get him."

Fazio's office was a room with two desks in it. The second desk was supposed to be for an officer of the same rank who had left five years ago and had never been replaced. "Shortage of personnel," the commissioner always replied whenever anyone submitted a written request for a replacement.

Fazio stood up, perplexed to see the inspector come in. It was rather rare for Montalbano to enter his room.

"Good morning, Chief. What's up? Want me to come to your office?"

"No. Since I want to report a crime, it's up to me to come to you."

"Report a crime?" Fazio grew even more perplexed.

"Yes. I want to report a breaking and entering and burglary. Or rather, a breaking and entering and attempted burglary. What's certain is the breaking. Of my balls, that is."

"I haven't understood a word, Chief."

"Burglars broke into my house, in Marinella."

"Burglars?"

"But they clearly weren't burglars."

"They weren't burglars?"

"Listen, Fazio, either you stop repeating what I say, or my mood is going to get decidedly irritable. Close your mouth, which is still hanging open, and sit down. That way I can sit down, too, and tell you the whole story."

Fazio sat down, stiff as a broomstick.

"So, one evening, Ingrid comes to my house and . . ." the inspector began, and he told him about the burglars' first entry and the disappearance of the watch.

"Well," said Fazio, "it sounds to me like a robbery — junkies needing to buy the next fix."

"Wait, there's a second part. This story comes in instalments. Yesterday afternoon, Ingrid came by at three in her car . . ."

This time, when the inspector had finished, Fazio remained silent.

"Aren't you going to say anything?"

"I was thinking. It's clear that the first time, they took the watch to make it look like they were burglars, but they didn't find what they were looking for. Since they had to come back a second time, they decided to lay their cards on the table and returned the watch. Maybe by giving back the watch they meant to say that they'd found what they were looking for and won't be back."

"But we don't know that with any certainty. One thing is certain, though: they're in a hurry to find what they're looking for. And if they haven't found it, they might try again, even today, or tonight, or tomorrow, at the latest."

"I've just thought of something," said Fazio.

"Out with it."

"Are you pretty sure they're spying on you?"

"Ninety per cent."

"What time does your housekeeper leave?"

"Around twelve-thirty, quarter to one."

"Could you call her and tell her you're going to come home for lunch today?"

"Yeah, sure. Why?"

"That way, you go home and eat lunch so that nobody can break in because you're there. At three o'clock, I'll come by with the squad car. I'll have the siren going and make a big racket. You come running out, get in the car, and we'll leave."

"Where to?"

"We'll go and visit the temples. If they are keeping an eye on you, they'll think I came to get you for an emergency. And they'll spring into action."

"So?"

"Well, the people who are spying on you won't know that Galluzzo's lurking nearby. In fact, I'll send him there right now and explain the situation to him."

"No, no, Fazio, there's no need — "

"Lemme tell you something, Chief. This whole thing smells funny to me, and I don't like it."

"But do you know what they're looking for?"

"What, you yourself don't know, and you want *me* to tell you?"

"When does the Giacomo Licco trial begin?"

"In about a week, I think. Why do you ask?"

Giacomo Licco had been arrested by Montalbano a while back. He was a Mafia lightweight, a shakedown thug for the protection racket. One day he shot at the legs of a shopkeeper who had refused to pay up. Scared to death, the shopkeeper had always maintained that it was a stranger who shot at him. The inspector, however, had found considerable evidence pointing to Giacomo Licco. The problem was that there was no telling how the trial would turn out, and Montalbano would have to testify.

"It's possible they're not looking for anything. Maybe it's a warning: *Watch what you say at the trial, because we can go in and out of your house as we please.*"

"That's also possible."

"Hello, Adelina?"

"Yes, signore."

"What are you doing?"

"I tryinna putta house beck in orda."

"Have you made something to eat?"

"I do that later."

"Do it now. I'm coming home for lunch at one."

"Whatteva you say, sir."

"What'd you get?"

"A coupla sole I gonna fry. An' pasta witta broccoli to start."

Fazio came in.

"Galluzzo's gone to Marinella. He knows a spot where he can hide and keep an eye on your house from the sea side."

"All right. Listen, don't talk about this with anyone, not even Mimì."

"OK."

"Have a seat. Is Augello in?"

"Yes, sir."

The inspector picked up the phone.

"Catarella, tell Inspector Augello I'd like to see him."

Mimì showed up at once.

"Yesterday I went to Fiacca," Montalbano began, "where there was a horse race. Mrs Esterman was one of the people running in it, on a horse lent to her by Lo Duca. This same Lo Duca spoke to me at length. In his opinion, the whole affair is a vendetta by a certain Gerlando Gurreri, a former groom in his employ. Have you ever heard his name before?"

"Never," Fazio and Augello said in a single voice.

"Whereas we ought to know more about him. Apparently he's taken up with some crooks. You want to look into it, Fazio?"

"All right."

"Are you going to tell us what Lo Duca told you, and in minute detail?" asked Mimì.

"Coming right up."

"It's not really such a far-fetched hypothesis," was Mimì's comment when the inspector had finished talking.

"I feel the same way," said Fazio.

"But if Lo Duca is right," said Montalbano, "do you realize that the investigation ends here?"

"Why's that?" asked Augello.

"Mimì, what Lo Duca told me, he has not told and will never tell our colleagues in Montelusa. All they have is a generic report of the theft of two horses. They don't know that one of them was bludgeoned to death, because we haven't told them. Besides, Mrs Esterman never even filed a report with us. And Lo Duca told me explicitly that he knew we were not in contact with Montelusa on this issue. Therefore, whatever way you look at it, we have no card in hand that tells us how to proceed."

"And so?"

"And so there are at least two things we need to do. The first is to find out more about Gerlando Gurreri. Mimì, you reproached me for believing Mrs Esterman's story without checking it out. Let's try to check out what Lo Duca told me, starting with his clubbing Gurreri in the head. Surely he must have been treated in some hospital in Montelusa, no?"

"I get it," said Fazio. "You want proof that Lo Duca's story is true."

"Right."

"Consider it done."

"The second thing is that there's one element of particular importance in Lo Duca's hypothesis. He told me that in reality nobody actually knows, at present, which of the two horses was killed — whether it was his or Esterman's. Lo Duca maintains this was done to make him stew in his own juices for a while. But one thing is certain, and that is that nobody really knows which horse it was. Lo Duca also told me that his horse

125

is called Rudy. Now, if there is a photograph of this horse, and if Fazio and I could see it . . ."

"I think I may know where to find one," said Mimì. He chuckled and then continued, "Certainly for somebody who's supposedly lost his wits, this Gurreri, based on what Lo Duca told you, can think very clearly."

"In what sense?"

"In the sense that first he kills Esterman's horse to put Lo Duca on tenterhooks concerning his own horse's fate, and then he phones Esterman so that Lo Duca can no longer hide from her the fact that her horse was stolen . . . To me he sounds sharp as a knife, this guy, and not like some poor brainless bastard!"

"I pointed this out to Lo Duca," said Montalbano.

"And what'd he say?"

"He said that most probably Gurreri is being advised by some of his accomplices."

"Hmph," said Mimì.

CHAPTER
TEN

He was about to leave to go home when the telephone rang.

"Chief? Chief? 'At'd be the lady Esther Mann for you."

"On the phone?"

"Yessir."

"Tell her I'm not here."

The instant he set down the receiver, the phone rang again.

"Chief, 'at'd be summon says 'e's Pasquale Cirribbicciò onna tiliphone."

It must be Pasquale Cirrinciò, one of Adelina the housekeeper's two sons, both of whom were thieves constantly in and out of jail. Montalbano, however, was made godfather of Pasquale's son at the baptism.

"What is it, Pasquà? Are you calling from prison?"

"No, sir, Inspector, I'm on house arrest."

"Is something wrong?"

"Inspector, my mother called me this morning and told me wha' happened."

Adelina had told her son that burglars had broken into Montalbano's house. The inspector didn't say a word, but waited to hear the rest.

"I wanted 'a tell you I called up a few o' my friends."

"Did you find anything out?"

"Just that my friends got nothing to do with it. One of 'em told me they wasn't so stupid as to go breakin' into a cop's house. So either it was done by outsiders or by a different circuit."

"Maybe a higher circuit?"

"I wouldn't know, sir."

"Very well, Pasquà. Thanks."

"Much obliged."

So, it was pretty clear now that burglars had nothing to do with this. And he didn't think it was outsiders, either. It had to be somebody else, who wasn't part of the "circuit", as Pasquale called it.

He laid the table on the veranda, warmed up the pasta with broccoli, and started eating. And as he was regaling himself, he had the distinct impression that he was being watched. Often another person's gaze has the same effect as hearing your name called: you hear the call, but you don't know where it came from, and so you start looking around.

He didn't see a living soul on the beach, aside from a limping dog. The morning fisherman had returned to land, his boat pulled ashore.

The inspector got up to fetch the sole from the kitchen, and at that moment he was nearly blinded by a flash of light that was there one second and gone the next. Surely it must have been a reflection of sunlight on glass. It had come from the direction of the sea.

But there were no windows or houses or cars on the sea, he thought.

Pretending to pick up the dirty dish, he leaned forward, looking up to see what he could see. At some distance from shore there was a stationary boat, but he was unable to tell how many men were on it. Once upon a time, however, when he was younger, he could even have said what colour their eyes were. Well, maybe not quite, but he surely would have seen better.

He kept a pair of binoculars in the house, but surely those who were spying on him from the boat also had a pair of binoculars and would immediately realize he had discovered them. It was best to behave as if he hadn't noticed anything.

He went inside and, a few minutes later, came back out on the veranda with the soles. He sat down and began eating them.

And, little by little, he became convinced that that boat had been out there ever since he first opened the French windows to lay the table. He had paid no mind to it, at the time. When he finished eating, it was already past two o'clock. He went into the bathroom to freshen up. Then he went back out on the veranda with a book in his hand, sat down, and lit a cigarette. The boat hadn't moved.

He began reading. Fifteen minutes later, he heard a siren approaching. He kept reading as if it had nothing to do with him. The sound grew louder until it stopped in the parking area in front of his house. From their position on the water, the people in the boat could see both the veranda and the parking area. He heard the doorbell ring.

He got up and went to open the door. Fazio had kept the light flashing on the roof of the car.

"Chief, there's an emergency."

Why was he hamming it up so much when there were just the two of them? Maybe Fazio thought there were some hidden microphones nearby? Come on!

"I'll be right with you."

Clearly the people on the boat had witnessed the whole scene. The inspector locked the French windows with the dead bolt, came outside, locked the front door, and got in the car.

Fazio turned the siren back on and screeched the tyres loud enough to make Galluzzo envious.

"I figured out where they're watching me from."

"And where's that?"

"From a boat. Think we ought to tell Galluzzo?"

"Maybe you're right. I'll ring him on his mobile."

Galluzzo answered immediately.

"Gallù, I wanted to tell you that the chief has worked out — Oh, yeah? OK, stay on the alert."

He turned off his phone and turned towards the inspector.

"Galluzzo had already worked out that the three guys on that boat were only pretending to be fishing and were really keeping your house under surveillance."

"But where is Galluzzo hiding?"

"Chief, you know the house that's been under construction for ten years, directly across the road from yours? Well, he's on the second floor."

"And where are you taking me?"

"Didn't we say we were gonna go and visit the temples?"

Before taking the panoramic road to the temples — which could only be travelled on foot, though they, being policemen, were allowed to go by car — Montalbano asked Fazio to stop, went into a bar-bookshop, and bought a guide.

"Are you serious? You really want to do the tour?"

No, he wasn't serious, not really. But the fact was that although he had been there many times, every time he went back he always forgot the period of construction, the dimensions, the number of columns . . .

"Let's go up to the top," said the inspector, "and we'll visit each temple as we make our way down."

Once at the top, they parked the car and climbed to the uppermost temple on foot.

The construction of the temple of Juno Lucina dates from 450 BC. It measures 41 metres in length and 19.55 in width, and used to have thirty-four columns . . .

They looked at it carefully, then got back in the car. They drove a few metres, pulled up and parked, then walked uphill to the second temple.

The Temple of Concord is dated 450 BC. It is 42.1 metres long, 19.7 metres wide and originally had thirty-four columns, each 6.83 metres high.

They looked at this, too, then got back in the car and did as before.

The Temple of Hercules is the most ancient. It dates from 520 BC. Measuring 73.4 metres in length and . . .

They looked at this one in detail.

"Are we gonna visit the other temples?"

"No," said Montalbano, who was already feeling fed up with archaeology. "What the hell is Galluzzo up to? It's been almost an hour!"

"If he hasn't called, it means he — "

"Ring him."

"No, Chief. What if he's close to your house and his phone starts ringing?"

"Then call Catarella and let me talk to him."

Fazio complied.

"Any news, Cat?"

"Nossir, Chief. But the lady Esther Mann called. She axed if you could call 'er."

Montalbano and Fazio spent another half hour pacing back and forth in front of the temple.

The inspector was growing more and more nervous. Fazio tried to distract him.

"Chief, why is the Temple of Concord almost intact but the others aren't?"

"Because there was an emperor, Theodosius, who ordered that all the pagan temples and sanctuaries should be destroyed, except for those that were being converted into Christian churches. And since the Temple of Concord became a Christian church, it was left standing. A fine example of tolerance. Just like today."

After this brief cultural digression, however, the inspector returned at once to the matter at hand.

132

"Want to bet those three in the boat were real fishermen? Listen, let's go to the bar and sit down."

This proved impossible. All the tables were occupied by English, German, French, and especially Japanese tourists, who were taking snapshots of anything they could think of, including a pebble that had found its way into one of their shoes. The inspector started cursing the saints.

"Let's get out of here," he said, agitated.

"Where we gonna go?"

"We'll go and scratch our balls in — "

At that moment, Fazio's mobile rang.

"It's Galluzzo," he said, bringing the little phone to his ear.

"OK, we'll be right there," he said immediately.

"What did he say?"

"He said we have to go immediately to your house."

"He didn't say anything else?"

"No, sir."

They drove back to Marinella at a speed that even Schumacher in a Formula One Grand Prix rarely achieved, but without flashing lights or siren. When they arrived, they found the front door open.

They raced inside.

In the dining room, one half of the French windows was dangling from its hinges.

Galluzzo, pale as death, was sitting on the sofa. He had drunk a glass of water and was holding the empty glass in his hand. He stood up as soon as he saw them.

"Are you all right?" Montalbano asked him, looking him straight in the eye.

"Yes, sir, but I got really scared."

"Why?"

"One of the two shot at me three times, but missed."

"Really? And what did you do?"

"I fired back. And I think I hit the one who hadn't shot. But the other guy, the one with the weapon, grabbed him and dragged him all the way to the road, where there was a car waiting for them."

"Feel up to telling us the whole story from the start?"

"Sure, I'm OK now."

"Would you like a little whisky?"

"That would be nice, Chief!"

Montalbano took the glass from his hand, poured him a generous serving, and gave it to him. Fazio, who had gone out onto the veranda, came back inside with a dark look on his face.

"After you two left, they waited half an hour before coming to shore," Galluzzo began.

"They wanted to be sure we had really left," said Fazio.

"But, once ashore, they hung around the boat for a long time, looking every which way. Then, after about an hour, two of them took a couple of big jerry cans out of the boat and started coming towards the house."

"What about the third guy?" asked Montalbano.

"The third guy started taking the boat out to sea again. So I ran out of my cover and took up a position behind the left corner of the house. When I looked around the corner, one of the guys, who was holding a crowbar in his hand, had just finished prising the

134

French window off its hinges. Then they went inside. As I was trying to figure out what to do, the two guys came back out on the veranda. I'm sure they were coming to get the jerry cans. I decided couldn't waste any more time. So I jumped out, pointed my gun at them, and said: 'Stop! Police!'

"Ah, Chief! In a flash, one of the two, the bigger guy, pulled out a gun and fired at me. I took cover behind the corner of the house. Then I saw that they were running away towards the parking area in front of the house, so I ran after them. And the big guy shot at me again. So I shot back and the other guy, who was running beside him, started staggering like he was drunk and fell to his knees. Then the big guy pulled him up with one arm and fired a third shot at me. When they got as far as the road, there was a car there with its doors open, and they sped away."

"So," Montalbano observed, "it was already planned that they would escape by land."

"Excuse me," Fazio said to Galluzzo, "but why didn't you keep running after them?"

"Because my pistol jammed," Galluzzo replied.

He took it out of his pocket and handed it to Fazio.

"Take it to weapons with my sincere thanks. If they'd realized I couldn't shoot anymore, I wouldn't be here telling you what happened."

Montalbano made as if to go out on the veranda.

"I already checked, Chief," said Fazio. "There are two twenty-litre jerry cans full of petrol. They were going to burn down your house."

Now, that was serious news.

"So, Chief, how should I proceed?" asked Galluzzo.

"About what?"

"About the two shots I fired. If the people at weapons ask me —"

"Tell them you had to shoot a rabid dog and the gun jammed."

"Just what, exactly, are your intentions, Chief?" asked Fazio.

"To have somebody fix the French windows," said the inspector, cool as a cucumber.

"If you want, I could fix it for you in less than an hour," said Galluzzo. "You got the tools?"

"Go and look in the storeroom."

"Chief," Fazio resumed, "we've got to agree on an explanation."

"Why?"

"'Cause in the next five minutes our guys, or the carabinieri, are liable to arrive."

"Why?" the inspector repeated.

"Was there or was there not an exchange of gunfire? Five shots were fired! Somebody in the area must surely have called the police or the — "

"How much you want to bet?"

"On what?"

"That nobody called anybody. Given the time of day, most of the people who heard the shots either thought it was a motorbike backfiring or somebody fooling around. The two or three who realized it was gunshots, being practical and smart, probably kept doing whatever the hell they were doing."

136

"There's everything I need here," said Galluzzo, returning with the tool drawer.

And he got down to work. After he had been hammering awhile, the inspector said to Fazio: "Let's go in the kitchen. You want some coffee?"

"Yeah, thanks."

"How about you, Gallù?"

"No, thanks, Chief. Otherwise I won't sleep tonight."

Fazio was silent, lost in thought.

"You worried?"

"Yeah, Chief. The boat, the car, the continuous surveillance, at least three men for the job . . . This isn't some casual thing. It stinks of the Mafia to me, if you really want to know. Maybe you were right to think of the Giacomo Licco trial."

"Fazio, I haven't got any of the papers on Licco here at home. And they realized that when they did their thorough search. If they came back today to set fire to the place, it must mean they want to intimidate me."

"That's what I'm saying."

"But are you convinced they're doing it for Licco's sake?"

"What other important stuff have you got going at the moment?"

"Important stuff, nothing."

"You see? Listen to me, Chief, it's the Cuffaros who are behind all this. Licco's one of theirs."

"And you think they would go to such lengths for a petty gangster like Licco?"

"Chief, petty or not, he's still their hood. They can't just drop him. If they don't protect him, they'll lose the trust of their members."

"But how could they possibly imagine that I would suddenly get scared, go to trial, and say, *I'm sorry, I made a mistake; Licco's got nothing to do with this.*"

"But that's not what they want! All they want is for you, at the trial, to seem a little uncertain. That'll be enough. As for picking apart your evidence, the Cuffaros' lawyers'll take care of that. And if you want some advice, I suggest you sleep at the station tonight."

"They aren't coming back, Fazio. My life is not in danger."

"What makes you so sure?"

"The simple fact that they waited till I had gone out to set fire to my house. If they wanted to kill me — aside from the fact that they could have picked me off from the boat at any time with a precision rifle — they would have lit the fire at night, when I was at home asleep."

Fazio thought about this for a moment.

"Maybe you're right. You're more useful to them alive."

But he seemed more doubtful than before.

"Chief, there's one thing I don't understand. Why don't you want to tell anyone about all this?"

"Think about it for a minute. Let's say I officially report breaking and entering and attempted burglary. Attempted, mind you, because I don't know whether they took anything or not. You know what will happen the very same day?"

138

"No, sir."

"The very second the evening news comes on Tele-Vigàta, the purse-lipped chicken-arse face of their commentator Pippo Ragonese will pop up and say: *Have you heard the news? Apparently burglars can come and go as they please with impunity at the house of Inspector Montalbano!* And I'll come out looking like a complete idiot."

"You're right. But you could go talk about it privately with the commissioner."

"With Bonetti-Alderighi?! You must be joking! He'll order me to proceed according to the rules! And I'll be hounded to death! No, Fazio, it's not that I don't want to do it; I *can't* do it."

"Whatever you say, sir. What are you going to do, go back to the station?"

Montalbano glanced at his watch. It was already past six.

"No, I think I'll stay here."

Half an hour later, Galluzzo triumphantly announced that he'd finished the repair and the French window was as good as new.

Adelina had succeeded in putting the living room back in order, but the bedroom was still in total disarray. All the drawers had been thrown open and their contents strewn about on the floor; they had even taken out all the suits hanging in the cupboard and turned all the pockets inside out.

Wait a second!

This meant that what they were looking for was something that could fit inside a pocket. A sheet of paper? A small object? No, a sheet of paper was probably the more likely hypothesis. Which brought him back to square one: the Licco trial. The phone rang, and he went to pick up.

"Diss 'Spector Montalbano?"

A deep voice, speaking heavy dialect.

"Yes."

"Do whatcha sposta do, idiot."

He hadn't time to respond before the caller hung up.

The first thing he thought was that they still had him under surveillance, since the phone call was made after Fazio and Galluzzo had left. But even if Fazio and Galluzzo had been there, what could they have done? Nothing at all. With his men there, however, the inspector would at least have felt less spooked. A subtle psychological tactic. At the other end, directing the whole thing, there must be somebody sharp as a knife, as Mimì had said.

The second thing he thought was that he could never do what he was supposed to do, in that he had utterly no idea what, according to the anonymous caller, he was supposed to do.

They should be a little clearer, dammit!

CHAPTER
ELEVEN

He went back into the bedroom to put things in order, and barely five minutes later the phone rang again. He picked up the receiver and spoke before the other could open his mouth.

"Listen here, you motherfucking son of a bitch."

"*What* is your problem?" Ingrid interrupted him.

"Oh, it's you. I'm sorry, I thought ... So, what's up?"

"Considering the greeting, I don't think you're in the right mood. But I'll try anyway. I only want to know why you won't return Rachele's phone calls ..."

"Did she tell you to ask me?"

"No, I'm doing this of my own initiative, after seeing how bad she felt. So, what is it?"

"You have to believe me, today has been the kind of day that — "

"Do you swear that's not just an excuse?"

"I won't swear to anything, but it's not an excuse."

"Well, that's a relief. I was thinking this was some Catholic rejection of the woman who led you into temptation."

"You really shouldn't put it in those terms."

"Why not?"

"Because, as you told me yourself, what took place between Rachele and me was a transaction, an exchange. If Mrs Esterman has no complaints concerning the matter — "

"No, no complaints. On the contrary."

"— then there's no reason to talk, don't you think?"

Ingrid seemed not to have heard.

"So I'll tell her to call you later at home?"

"No. Tomorrow morning would be better, in my office. Now I have to . . . go out."

"So you'll talk to her when she calls?"

"I promise."

After two hours of toil, of stooping and standing, grabbing and folding, pushing and pulling, the bedroom was back to normal.

And now he should eat something, except that he wasn't hungry.

He sat down on the veranda and lit a cigarette.

All at once he realized that, sitting there as he was, with the veranda's light on, he made a perfect target, especially as it was a very dark night. But the reason he had told Fazio that he was certain they had no intention of killing him was not so much to reassure him, but because he was deeply convinced of it. So convinced that he had even left his pistol, as usual, in the glove compartment of his car.

Anyway, if they decided to start shooting at him, how was he going to defend himself? With a pistol that probably risked jamming after the first shot, like Galluzzo's, against three Kalashnikovs?

By going to spend the night at the station, as Fazio had suggested? Come on!

The moment he left the building to go out to eat or have a coffee at the bar, the usual motorcyclist in helmet and visor could increase his body weight with a few pounds of lead.

Go around with an escort at all times? But, as had amply been proved, an escort had never succeeded in preventing a murder.

If anything, all it had ever accomplished was an increase in the number of dead: not just the designated victim, but two or three men from the escort as well.

And this was inevitable. Because anyone who comes up to you to kill you knows exactly what he needs to do and has likely rehearsed the scenario dozens of times, whereas the men in the escort, who are trained to fire on the rebound — that is, after they've been attacked, and thus defensively, not offensively — know nothing of the intentions of the man who is approaching. A few seconds later, when they finally understand, it is already too late: that difference of a few seconds between the attacker and the escort is the killer's winning card.

In short, the brain of the person using a weapon to kill has one more gear than the one who uses it to defend.

At any rate, the inspector felt on edge, there was no denying it.

On edge, not afraid.

And also deeply offended.

When he'd seen the house turned upside down, his first feeling was shame. The comparison was, of course, untenable, but in a vague way he understood why very often a woman who has been raped feels too humiliated to report it.

His house — in other words, his person — had been brutally violated, searched, turned inside out by unknown hands. In fact, the only way he'd been able to talk about it with Fazio was to pretend he was joking. The rifling through all his belongings had upset him considerably more than the attempt to burn the house down.

Then there was that offensive telephone call. But it wasn't so much the tone or the final insult. The offence lay in the fact that someone could think that he was the kind of man to give in to intimidation and do the bidding of others, like some measly thug or worthless nobody. Had he ever given them any reason, any hint in his actions or words, to have such an opinion of him?

Whatever the case, these people surely were not about to stop. They even showed signs of being in a hurry.

Do what you're supposed to do.

Maybe Fazio was right. Everything that was happening to him must have some connection to the Licco trial. In the reconstruction of events the inspector had presented to send Licco to prison, there was one weak link, he remembered. But he was unable to bring it into focus. Surely Licco's lawyers had noticed this weak point and discussed it with the Cuffaros, who had then sprung into action.

144

The first thing he had to do in the morning was get hold of the Licco file and reread it.

The telephone rang. He let it ring. A minute later, it stopped ringing. If they were out there watching him, they would see that he was taking things easy. He wouldn't even get up to answer the phone.

When sleep started to come over him and he went back inside, he decided to leave the French windows ajar. That way, if they were planning to pay him a visit during the night, they wouldn't have to break them a third time.

He went to the bathroom, lay down in bed, but no sooner had he slipped between the sheets than the phone rang again. This time he got up and answered it.

It was Livia.

"Why didn't you answer the first time?"

"What first time?"

"About an hour ago."

So it was her who had called.

"Maybe I was in the shower and didn't hear."

"Are you all right?"

"Yes. And you?"

"I'm fine. I wanted to ask you something."

That made two. First Ingrid, and now Livia. All the women had questions to ask him. Ingrid he had answered with a half lie. Would he have to do the same with Livia? He coined a new proverb: *A hundred lies a day / keeps all the women at bay.*

"Go ahead."

"Are you busy in the next few days?"

"Not exceedingly."

145

"I really feel like coming to Marinella to spend a few days with you. I could catch the plane at three o'clock tomorrow aftern — "

"No!"

He must have yelled it.

"Thank you!" said Livia, after a pause.

And she hung up.

Matre santa! Now, how was he going to explain to her that that "No!" had escaped him because he was afraid to involve her in the nasty affair in which he was buried up to his neck?

What if they got it in their heads to start shooting when Livia was with him, just to make a point? No, there was no way. Having Livia about the house at that moment was a terrible idea.

He called her back. He was expecting her not to answer, but she actually picked up.

"Just because I'm curious."

"About what?"

"To see whether you can manage to justify the way you said no."

"I can see how you would be upset. But you have to understand, Livia, these are not excuses, you have to believe me. The fact is that in the last few days, burglars have broken into my house three times, and I — "

Livia started laughing uncontrollably.

What the fuck was so funny about it? Eh? You tell her that burglars go in and out of your house whenever the hell they feel like it, and not only does she not say anything to comfort you, she thinks it's comical? How thoughtful! He started to feel angry.

146

"Listen, Livia, I don't see what — "

"Burglars breaking into the home of the famous Inspector Montalbano! Ha ha ha!"

"If you would just calm down a second . . ."

"Ha ha ha ho ho ho!"

What to do? Hang up? Wait it out? Luckily she started calming down.

"I'm sorry, but it seems so funny to me!"

Which was exactly the reaction other people would have if it came to be known about town.

"Let me tell you what happened. It's a strange story. Because, you know, they came back again this afternoon."

"What did they steal?"

"Nothing."

"Nothing? Tell me!"

"Three days ago, Ingrid had come here for dinner . . ."

He bit his tongue, but it was too late. The damage was done.

At the other end of the line, the barometer must have signalled a gathering storm. Ever since the situation between them had returned to normal, Livia had been in the grips of a jealousy the likes of which she had never felt before.

"And since when have you been in the habit?"

"What habit?"

"The habit of the two of you having dinner in Marinella. By moonlight. Speaking of which, do you light a candle on the table?"

It ended badly.

★ ★ ★

And therefore, whether from the aggravation of the visit by the three men who wanted to burn down his house, or from the aggravation of the anonymous phone call, or from the aggravation of the squabble with Livia, he ended up sleeping hardly at all, and the little he did sleep was broken up into spells of twenty minutes or so. He woke up in a complete stupor. A half-hour shower and a half pint of espresso put him at least in a condition to tell his right hand from his left.

"I'm not here for anyone," he said as he passed in front of Catarella's station.

Catarella came running after him.

"Not here telephonically or poissonally?"

"I'm not here, can you get that through your head?"

"Not even for the c'mishner?"

For Catarella, the c'mishner was only one grade below the Almighty.

"Not even."

He went into his office, locked the door, and after half an hour of cursing, found the file on his investigation of Giacomo Licco.

He studied it for two hours, taking notes.

Then he phoned Prosecutor Giarrizzo, who would be representing the state at the Licco trial.

"Inspector Montalbano here. I'd like to speak to Prosecutor Giarrizzo."

"Dr Giarrizzo is at the courthouse. He'll be busy all morning," replied a female voice.

"Could you tell him to call me when he gets back? Thanks."

148

He put the sheet of paper with his notes in his pocket, then picked up the receiver again.

"Catarella, is Fazio here?"

"'E in't onna premisses, Chief."

"What about Augello?"

"'E's 'ere."

"Tell him to come to my office."

Remembering he had locked the door, he got up, opened it, and found Mimì Augello standing in front of him with a magazine in his hand.

"Why'd you lock yourself in?"

Just because you do something, what gives others the right to ask why you did it? He hated this kind of question. Ingrid: Why won't you call Rachele back? Livia: Why didn't you answer the first time I called? And now Mimì.

"Just between us, Mimì, I had half a mind to hang myself, but now that you're here . . ."

"Ah, well, if that's your intention — which, incidentally, I approve of, unconditionally — then I'll leave at once and you can continue."

"Come in and sit down."

Mimì noticed the file of the Licco trial on the desk.

"You reviewing your lesson?"

"Yes. You got any news?"

"Yes. This magazine."

And he set it down on the inspector's desk. It was a glossy, luxurious bimonthly magazine that oozed with the money of its contributors. It was called *The Province*, with the subtitle *Art, Sport, and Beauty*.

Montalbano skimmed through it. Horrific paintings by amateur painters who considered themselves, at the very least, on a par with Picasso, ignoble poems signed by poetesses with double surnames (provincial poetesses always do this), the life and miracles of a certain Montelusan who had become deputy mayor of some lost town in Canada, and, lastly, in the sports section, no less than five pages devoted to "Saverio Lo Duca and His Horses".

"What's the article say?"

"Crap. But you were interested in a photo of the stolen horse, no? It's the third one. And which horse did Mrs Esterman ride?"

"Moonbeam."

"He's the one in the fourth shot."

The photos were large and in colour, and each had the name of the horse as its caption.

To have a better look, Montalbano reached into a drawer and pulled out a large magnifying glass.

"You look like Sherlock Holmes," said Mimì.

"So would that make you Dr Watson?"

He could see no difference between the dead horse on the beach and the one in the photograph. But he didn't know the first thing about horses. The only hope was to phone Rachele, but he didn't want to do this in Mimì's presence. She was liable to bring up some dangerous subjects, thinking him alone.

But as soon as Augello left to go back to his own office, the inspector called Rachele's mobile.

"Montalbano here."

"Salvo! Lovely! I phoned you this morning but they said you weren't there."

He had forgotten he'd solemnly promised Ingrid to call Rachele back. He would have to fire off another lie.

In his mind he coined another proverb: *Often a lie / will help you get by.*

"In fact I wasn't here. But the minute I got back and was told you had asked for me, I called you."

"I don't want to take up your time. Is there any news on the investigation?"

"Which one?"

"The one into the killing of my horse, naturally!"

"But we're not conducting any investigation into that, since you never filed a report."

"You're not?" said Rachele, disappointed.

"No. If anything, you should talk to Montelusa Central. That's where Lo Duca reported the theft of the two horses."

"I was hoping that — "

"I'm sorry. Listen, I've just happened, purely by chance, to come across a magazine that has a photograph of the horse of Lo Duca's that was stolen — "

"Rudy."

"Right. To me Rudy looks identical to the dead horse I saw on the beach."

"Of course, they did look a lot alike. But they weren't identical. My horse, Super, for example, had a strange little spot, a sort of three-pointed star, on his left flank. Did you see it?"

"No, because that was the side he was lying on."

"That's why they came and took him away. So he couldn't be identified. I'm more and more convinced that Chichi is right: they wanted to make him stew in his own juices."

"It's possible . . ."

"Listen . . ."

"Tell me."

"I'd like . . . to talk to you. To see you."

"Rachele, you've got to believe me, I'm not lying when I say you've caught me at a very difficult moment."

"But you have to eat to survive, don't you?"

"Well, yes. But I don't like to talk when I eat."

"I'll talk to you for only five minutes, I promise, after we've finished eating. Could we meet this evening?"

"I don't know yet. Let's do this. Call me here, at my office, at eight o'clock sharp, and I'll give you an answer."

He picked up the Licco file again, reread it, and jotted down a few more notes. He reviewed and re-reviewed the arguments that he had used against Licco, reading them with the eyes of a defence lawyer, and what he remembered as a weak point now no longer seemed like a slight break in the fabric but a gaping hole. Licco's friends were right. His attitude on the stand would be decisive; he needed only display a hint of hesitation and the lawyers would turn that hole into an out-and-out breach through which Licco could blithely walk away to a chorus of apologies on the part of the law.

152

When he came out of his office around one o'clock to go to the trattoria, Catarella called him.

"Beck y'pardon, Chief, but are you here or not?"

"Who's on the line?"

"Proxecutor Giarrazzo."

"Let me talk to him."

"Hello, Montalbano, this is Giarrizzo. You were looking for me?"

"Yes, thanks. I need to talk to you."

"Could you come to my office . . . wait . . . around five-thirty?"

In view of the fact that he had practically fasted the previous day, he decided to compensate.

"Enzo, I've got a really big appetite."

"Glad to hear it, Inspector. What can I bring you?"

"You know what I say? I think I'd have trouble deciding."

"Leave it to me."

After eating and eating, at a certain point he realized a wafer-thin mint would have been enough to make him explode, like that character in Monty Python's *The Meaning of Life*, a film he had found very funny. But it also occurred to him that it was his nervous agitation that had made him eat so much.

After strolling along the jetty for a good half hour, he returned to the office, but he still felt too much ballast in the hold. Fazio was waiting for him.

"Any news last night?" was the first thing he asked the inspector.

"Nothing. And what have you been doing?"

"I went to Montelusa Hospital. And I wasted the whole morning. Nobody wanted to tell me anything."

"Why not?"

"Privacy laws, Chief. And on top of that, I had no written authorization."

"So you've got nothing to show for it?"

"Who ever said that?" said Fazio, pulling a small sheet of paper out of his pocket.

"Where'd you get this information?"

"From a cousin of the uncle of a cousin of mine, who I found out works at the hospital."

Family relations, even those so distant that they would no longer be considered such in any other part of Italy, were often, in Sicily, the only way to obtain information, expedite a bureaucratic procedure, find the whereabouts of a missing person, land a job for an unemployed son, pay less taxes, get free tickets to movies, and so many other things that it was probably safer not to reveal to people who were not family.

154

CHAPTER
TWELVE

"So, Gerlando Gurreri, born in Vigàta on — " Fazio began, reading from his little piece of paper.

Montalbano cursed, leapt to his feet, leaned forward over the desk, and snatched the paper out of his hands. And as Fazio stood there in shock, he rolled it up into a little ball and tossed it into the wastebasket. He couldn't stand to listen to these records-office litanies Fazio was so fond of, which reminded him of nothing so much as the intricate genealogies of the Bible: Japhet, son of Joseph, begat fourteen children, Rachel, Ibrahim, Lot, Axanagor . . .

"How am I going to go on now?" asked Fazio.

"You can tell me what you remember."

"But when I've finished, can I have my piece of paper back?"

"All right."

Fazio seemed reassured.

"Gurreri is forty-six years old, and married with . . . now I don't remember. I had it written down on that paper. He lives in Vigàta at Via Nicotera 38 — "

"Fazio, I'm telling you for the last time: forget the vital statistics."

"OK, OK. Gurreri was treated at Montelusa Hospital in early February 2003. I don't remember the exact date, 'cause I had it written down on — "

"Fuck the exact date. And if you dare try again to remember something you'd written down, I'm going to take that little piece of paper out of the wastebasket and make you eat it."

"All right, all right. Gurreri was unconscious and brought in by a guy whose name I can't remember but had written down on — "

"Now I'm going to shoot you."

"I'm sorry, it just slipped out. This guy worked with Gurreri at Lo Duca's stable. He stated that Gurreri had been accidentally struck by a heavy iron bar, the one used to bolt the door to the stable. To cut a long story short, the doctors were forced to drill a hole in his skull, or something like that, because a huge haematoma was pressing against his brain. The operation was a success, but Gurreri was left disabled."

"How so?"

"He started suffering lapses of memory, fainting spells, sudden fits of anger, things like that. I was told Lo Duca paid for specialized care, but you couldn't really say there was any improvement."

"Actually the situation got worse, if anything, the way Lo Duca tells it."

"So that's as far as the hospital's concerned. But there are other things as well."

"Such as?"

"Before going to work for Lo Duca, Gurreri had a few years of jail time under his belt."

156

"Oh, yeah?"

"You bet. Burglary and attempted murder."

"Not bad."

"This afternoon I'm going to try to find out what people in town say about him."

"Good. Get going."

"'Scuse me, Chief, but could I retrieve my little piece of paper?"

The inspector headed off to Montelusa at four-thirty. After he'd been on the road for ten minutes or so, somebody behind him honked his horn. Montalbano pulled over to let him pass, but the other moved along slowly, pulled up beside him, and said:

"You've got a flat tyre, you know."

Matre santa! What was he going to do now? He had never managed to change a tyre in his life! Luckily, at that moment he spotted a car of carabinieri driving by. He raised his left arm, and they pulled over.

"You need anything?"

"Yes, thank you. Thank you very, very much. The name's Galluzzo, a surveyor by trade. If you would be so kind as change my rear left tyre for me . . ."

"You don't know how to do it?"

"Yes, I do, but unfortunately I have only limited mobility in my right arm and can't lift heavy objects."

"We'll take care of it."

He arrived at Giarrizzo's office ten minutes late.

"Sorry I'm late, doctor, but the traffic . . ."

157

Forty-year-old Nicola Giarrizzo, public prosecutor for the city of Montelusa, was a massive man, nearly six and a half feet tall and nearly six and a half feet wide, who, when he spoke to someone, liked to pace back and forth in the room, with the result that he was continually crashing into a chair one minute, an open window the next, or his own desk the next. Not because his eyesight was defective or because he was distracted, but simply because the space of an office of normal size was insufficient for him. He was like an elephant in a telephone booth.

After the inspector explained the reason for his visit, the prosecutor remained silent for a minute. Then he said:

"I think you're a little late."

"For what?"

"For coming to me to express your doubts."

"But you see —"

"And even if you'd come to express absolute certainty, you would still be too late."

"But why, may I ask?"

"Because by now everything that needed to be written has already been written."

"But I came to talk, not to write."

"It's the same thing. At this point, nothing will change anything. There will certainly be some new discoveries, big discoveries, which will come out over the course of the trial, but not until then. Is that clear?"

"Absolutely. And, in fact, I came to tell you — "

Giarrizzo raised a hand and stopped him.

"Among other things, I don't think your way of going about this is terribly correct. Don't forget, you, until proved otherwise, are also a witness."

It was true. And Montalbano absorbed the blow. He stood up, mildly angry. He'd made a fool of himself.

"Well, in that case — "

"What are you doing? Leaving? Are you upset?"

"No, but — "

"Sit down," said the prosecutor, crashing into the door, which had been left open.

The inspector sat down.

"Can we speak in a purely theoretical mode?" asked Giarrizzo.

What on earth was a "theoretical mode"? For lack of a better option, Montalbano consented.

"All right."

"So, to repeat, theoretically speaking, rhetorically, that is, let us posit the case of a certain police inspector, whom we shall henceforth call Martinez . . ."

Montalbano didn't like the name the prosecutor wanted to give him.

"Couldn't we call him something else?"

"But that's an utterly insignificant detail! However, if it means so much to you, please propose a name more to your liking," said Giarrizzo, irritated and crashing into a filing cabinet.

D'Angelantonio? DeGubernatis? Filippazzo? Cosentino? Aromatis? The names that came into the inspector's mind didn't sound right. So he gave up.

"All right, we can keep Martinez."

"So, let us posit that this Martinez, who has been conducting, and so on and so forth, the investigation into an individual we shall call Salinas — "Why the hell was Giarrizzo so fixated on Spanish names? "Is Salinas all right with you? — who is accused of having shot a shop owner and so on and so forth, realizes and so on and so forth that the case has a weak link and so on and so forth — "

"Excuse me, but *who* realizes the case has a weak link?" asked Montalbano, whose head was spinning with all the and so on and so forths.

"Martinez, no? The shop owner, whom we'll call — "

"Alvarez del Castillo," Montalbano promptly piped up.

Giarrizzo looked a little doubtful.

"Too long. Let's call him simply Alvarez. The shop owner Alvarez, however — though openly contradicting himself — claims not to recognize Salinas as the gunman. You with me so far?"

"I'm with you."

"On the other hand, Salinas claims to have an alibi, which, however, he doesn't want to reveal to Martinez. And so the inspector continues straight down his road, convinced that the reason Salinas doesn't want to reveal his alibi is that he hasn't got one. Is the picture clear?"

"Quite. At this point, however, I — I mean, Martinez begins to doubt: what if Salinas really does have an alibi, and pulls it out at the trial?"

"But this has already occurred to the people in charge of confirming the arrest and bringing the

160

accused to justice!" said Giarrizzo, tripping over a rug and threatening to collapse on top of the inspector, who for a moment feared being squashed to death under the Colossus of Rhodes.

"And how have they resolved the question?"

"With supplementary investigations concluded three months ago."

"But I never — "

"Martinez wasn't assigned this task because he'd already done his part. To conclude: Salinas's alibi is apparently a woman, his mistress, whose company he was in at the moment that Alvarez was shot."

"I'm sorry, but if Lic — I mean, Salinas really does have an alibi, it means the trial will end in — "

"A conviction!" said Giarrizzo.

"Why?"

"Because when Salinas's lawyers decide to pull out this alibi, the prosecution will know how to pick it apart. The defence, moreover, is unaware that the prosecution already knows the name of the woman who is supposed to provide this belated alibi."

"Mind telling me who she is?"

"You? But you, Inspector Montalbano, have nothing to do with this! If anything, it should be Martinez asking that question."

He sat down, wrote something on a sheet of paper, stood up, and held out his hand to Montalbano, who, bewildered, shook it.

"It was a pleasure to talk to you," said the prosecutor. "I'll see you at the trial."

He got up to leave, crashed into the half-closed door, knocking it partially off its hinges, and went out.

Still stunned, the inspector bent down to look at the sheet of paper on the desk. It had a name written on it: *Concetta Siragusa*.

He raced back to Vigàta, went to the station, and said to Catarella as he was passing by:

"Call Fazio on his mobile."

He barely had time to sit down before the telephone rang.

"What is it, Chief?"

"Drop everything you're doing and come here at once."

"I'm on my way."

It was now clear that he and Fazio had gone down the wrong path.

The investigation into Licco's alibi had been assigned not to him, Montalbano, but surely to the carabinieri, at the instruction of Giarrizzo. And equally surely, the Cuffaros had learned of the existence of this investigation by the men in black.

This meant that whatever behaviour he displayed in court, it would never have the slightest influence on the outcome of the trial.

Therefore all the pressure exerted on him — the ransacking of his house, the attempted arson, the anonymous phone call — had nothing to do with the Licco affair. So what, then, did they want from him?

162

Fazio listened in absolute silence to the conclusions the inspector had drawn after his chat with Giarrizzo.

"Maybe you're right," he said at the end.

"No 'maybe' about it."

"We'll have to wait to see what their next move is, after they failed to burn down your house."

Montalbano slapped his forehead.

"They've already made their move! I forgot to tell you!"

"What'd they do?"

"I got an anonymous phone call."

And he repeated the message to Fazio.

"The problem is, you don't know what it is they want you to do."

"Let's hope that their next move, as you say, will give us some idea. Have you managed to find out anything else about Gurreri?"

"Yes, but . . ."

"But what?"

"I need more time. I'd like to confirm it."

"Tell me anyway."

"Apparently he was recruited about three months ago."

"By whom?"

"The Cuffaros. Apparently they took on Gurreri to replace Licco."

"About three months ago, you say?"

"Yes. Is that important?"

"I don't know yet, but these same three months keep popping up. Three months ago, Gurreri left his house;

three months ago, the name of Licco's mistress was discovered, the one who will provide Licco's alibi; three months ago, Gurreri was recruited by the Cuffaros . . . Oh, I don't know."

"If you don't have anything else to tell me," said Fazio, standing up, "I'm going to go back and talk to a lady who's a neighbour of Gurreri's wife, who hates her guts. She had started telling me something, but then you rang me and I had to drop everything."

"Had she already told you anything?"

"Yeah. She said Concetta Siragusa, for the last few months —"

Montalbano leapt to his feet, eyes popping.

"What did you say?"

Fazio almost got scared.

"Wha'd I say, Chief?"

"Repeat it!"

"That Concetta Siragusa, Gurreri's wife — "

"Holy fucking shit!" said the inspector, falling heavily back into the chair.

"Chief, you're getting me worried! What is it?"

"Wait, let me recover."

He lit a cigarette. Fazio got up and shut the door.

"First, I want to know something," said the inspector. "You were telling me the neighbour lady told you that for the last few months Gurreri's wife . . . And that's where I interrupted you. Now continue."

"The neighbour was telling me that for some time now Gurreri's wife has seemed scared of her own shadow."

"Do you want to know how long Gurreri's wife has been scared?"

"Sure. Do you know?"

"For three months, Fazio. Exactly three months."

"But how do you know these things about Concetta Siragusa?"

"I don't know anything, but I can easily imagine them. And now I'll tell you how it all went. Three months ago, someone from the Cuffaro clan approaches Gurreri, who's a small-time crook, and asks him to join the family. He can't believe it; it's like getting a permanent employment contract after years of temping."

"But wait a second, if I may. What use could the Cuffaros possibly have for someone like Gurreri, who's not even all there in the head?"

"I'll get to that. The Cuffaros, however, impose a rather exacting condition on Gurreri."

"Namely?"

"That Concetta Siragusa, his wife, provide an alibi for Licco."

This time it was Fazio's turn to be shocked.

"Who told you that that Siragusa is Licco's mistress?"

"Giarrizzo. But he didn't tell me her name; he wrote it down on a sheet of paper, which he pretended to leave on his desk."

"But what's it mean?"

"It means that the Cuffaros don't give a flying fuck about Gurreri. It's his wife they want. Who, at a certain point, is forced to play ball, willy-nilly, even though she's scared out of her wits. At the same time, the Cuffaros tell Gurreri that it's best if he leaves his house; they'll take care of finding him a safe place to stay."

He torched another cigarette. Fazio went and opened the window.

"And since Gurreri, who now feels strong with the Cuffaros behind him, still wants to take revenge on Lo Duca, the family decides to lend him a hand. It's the Cuffaros, not a loser like Gurreri, who staged the horse operation. So, to conclude: for the past three months, Licco has had the alibi he didn't have before, and in the meanwhile, Gurreri has had the revenge he wanted. And they all lived happily ever after."

"And we —"

"And we take it up the you-know-what. But I'll tell you another thing," Montalbano continued.

"Tell me."

"At a certain point, Licco's lawyers will call Gurreri as a witness. You can bet on that. In one way or another they'll get him to talk on the stand. And Gurreri will swear that he has always known that his wife was Licco's mistress, and that this was why he left his home in disgust, fed up with the constant quarrels with Concetta, who wouldn't stop crying for her beau behind bars."

"Well, if that's the way it is —"

"How else could it be?"

"— maybe you'd best go back to Giarrizzo."

"What for?"

"To tell him what you've just told me."

"I'm not going back there, not even with a gun to my head . . . First of all, because he pointed out to me that it's improper for me to talk to him. And, secondly, because he has assigned the supplementary investigation to the carabinieri. Let him sort things out with them. Now hurry back and finish your discussion with Concetta's neighbour."

At eight o'clock on the dot, the phone rang.

"Chief, that'd be the lady Esther Mann."

Their date! He had completely forgotten about it! What was he going to do now? Should he say yes or no? He picked up the receiver, still undecided.

"Salvo? This is Rachele. Have you overcome your reservations?"

There was an ever so slight note of irony in her voice, which irritated him.

"I still haven't finished here."

You want to get wise with me? Then stew in your own juices.

"Think you'll manage to get away?"

"Well, I don't know. Maybe in an hour or so . . . But that's probably too late for you to go out to eat."

He was hoping she would say that in that case it was better to meet another evening. Instead, she said:

"OK, no problem. I can even eat at midnight, if need be."

O matre santa! How the hell was he going to spend the next hour with nothing to do in the office? Why had he played so hard to get? Most importantly, he was ravenous, eaten alive by his hunger.

"Wait. Can you hold on a second?"

"Of course."

He set the receiver down on the desk, got up, went over to the window, and pretended to be talking audibly to someone.

"What do you mean, you can't find it? . . . Put it off till tomorrow morning? . . . Well, all right."

He turned round to go back to his desk, but then froze. Standing in the doorway was Catarella, who looked at him with an expression between concern and fear.

"You feel OK, Chief?"

Without saying a word, Montalbano shot out one arm to signal that he should leave the room at once. Catarella disappeared.

"Rachele? Luckily I've managed to break free. Where should we meet?"

"Wherever you like."

"Have you got a car?"

"Ingrid lent me hers."

How ready Ingrid was to facilitate his encounters with Rachele!

"Why, doesn't she need it?"

"No, a friend of hers picked her up and will bring her home later."

He told her where they should meet. Before leaving the room, he picked up the magazine that Mimì Augello had brought him. It might help him rein in Rachele, if their conversation began to take a dangerous turn.

CHAPTER
THIRTEEN

Arriving at the Marinella Bar, he noticed that Ingrid's car was nowhere to be seen. Apparently Rachele was running late. She hardly had the same Swiss precision as her friend. He remained undecided as to whether he should wait for her outside or inside the bar. He felt a little uneasy about the encounter, there was no denying it. The fact was that, at fifty-six years and counting, never in his life had he met a woman — one, moreover, entirely foreign to him — after having had hasty, er, *sexual congress* with her, as Prosecutor Tommaseo might call it. And the real reason he hadn't wanted to return her phone calls was that he felt quite awkward talking to her. Awkward and a little ashamed to have shown this woman a side of himself that wasn't really him.

What should he say to her? How should he behave? What sort of expression should he wear?

To steel himself a little, he got out of his car, entered the establishment, walked up to the bar, and asked Pino, the barman, for a whisky, neat.

He had just finished downing it when he saw Pino's face drop. Eyes fixed on the entrance, the barman was an open-mouthed statue, like Lou Ravi in a crèche, a glass in one hand, a tea towel in the other.

The inspector turned around.

Rachele had just walked in.

She was so elegantly dressed, it was frightening. But her beauty was even more frightening.

It was as if her presence had suddenly increased the wattage of the lights in the bar. Pino was frozen, unable to move.

The inspector went up to greet her. And she proved very much the lady.

"Hello," she said, smiling at him, her blue eyes sparkling with genuine pleasure at seeing him. "Here I am."

And she made no move to kiss him or be kissed by proffering her cheek.

Montalbano was overwhelmed by a wave of gratitude, and immediately felt at ease.

"Care for an aperitif?"

"I'd rather not."

Montalbano forgot to pay for the whisky. Pino was still in the same position, spellbound. In the car park, Rachele asked:

"Have you decided where we're going?"

"Yes. To Montereale Marina."

"That's on the road to Fiacca, isn't it? Shall we take your car or Ingrid's?"

"Let's take Ingrid's. Would you mind driving? I feel a bit tired."

It wasn't true, but he could already feel the effect of the whisky. How could two fingers of whisky possibly make his head spin? Maybe it was the mix of whisky and Rachele that was so deadly?

They drove off. Rachele drove with assurance. She went fast, naturally, but maintained a constant speed. It took them ten minutes to get to Montereale.

"Now show me the way," she said.

Suddenly, again from the effect of that deadly mix, the inspector couldn't remember how to get there.

"I think you have to turn to the right."

The road on the right, which was not paved, came to an end in front of a farmhouse.

"Then turn around and take the road on the left."

That wasn't the right one, either, as it ended in front of the warehouse of the farmers' cooperative.

"Maybe we need to go straight," Rachele concluded.

And that, indeed, proved to be the right way.

Another ten minutes later, they were seated at a table in a restaurant where the inspector had been several times before and always eaten well.

The table they chose was under a pergola, at the edge of the beach. The sea was some thirty paces away, ever so lightly lapping the shore, making it clear that it had little desire to move. The stars were out, and there was not a cloud in the sky.

At another table sat two men of about fifty. On one of them the sight of Rachele had a quasi-lethal effect: the wine he was drinking went down the wrong way, and he nearly died choking. His friend finally managed, *in extremis*, to help him regain his breath, by dint of a series of powerful slaps on the back.

"They serve a white wine here that makes a nice aperitif as well . . ." said Montalbano.

"If you'll join me."

"Of course I will. Are you hungry?"

"On the way down to Marinella from Montelusa I wasn't, but I am now. It must be the sea air."

"I'm glad. I must confess that I'm always put off by women who don't like to eat because they're afraid to gain . . ."

He stopped short. Why was he suddenly speaking so confidentially with Rachele? What was happening?

"I've never followed diets," said Rachele. "So far, at least, I've never needed to, luckily."

The waiter brought the wine. They downed their first glasses.

"This is really good," said Rachele.

A couple about thirty years old walked in, looking around for a table. But as soon as the girl saw how her partner was eyeing Rachele, she took him by the arm and led him back indoors.

The waiter reappeared and, refilling the empty glasses, asked what they wanted to eat.

"Will you be having a first course or an antipasto?"

"Does the one exclude the other?" Rachele asked in turn.

"They serve fifteen different kinds of antipasto here," said Montalbano. "Which, frankly, I recommend."

"Fifteen?"

"Maybe more."

"All right, then. Antipasto it is."

"And for the main course?" asked the waiter.

172

"We'll decide that later," said Montalbano.

"Shall I bring another bottle with the antipasti?"

"I think you should."

A few minutes later, there wasn't any room left on the table for so much as a needle.

Shrimps, langoustine, flying squid, smoked tuna, fried balls of *nunnatu*, sea urchins, mussels, clams, octopus morsels *a strascinasale*, octopus morsels *affucati*, tiny fried squid, squid and cuttlefish tossed in a salad with orange slices and celery, capers wrapped in anchovies, sardines *a beccafico*, swordfish carpaccio . . .

The total silence in which they ate, occasionally exchanging glances of appreciation for the flavours and aromas, was interrupted only once, at the moment of transition to the anchovy-wrapped capers, when Rachele asked:

"Is something wrong?"

And Montalbano, feeling himself blush, said:

"No."

For the previous few minutes he had been lost watching her mouth open and close, the fork going in, revealing for an instant the intimacy of a palate as pink as a cat's, the fork coming out empty but still clasped by glistening teeth, the mouth closing again, the lips moving lightly, rhythmically, as she chewed. The mere sight of her mouth left one speechless. In a flash Montalbano remembered the evening in Fiacca, when he fell under the spell of those lips by the light of her cigarette.

When they had finished the antipasti, Rachele said:

"Good God!"

And she heaved a long sigh.

"Everything all right?"

"Couldn't be better."

The waiter came to remove the dishes.

"And what would you like as a main course?"

"Couldn't we wait a little?" Rachele asked.

"As you wish."

The waiter walked away. Rachele remained silent. Then, all at once, she grabbed her packet of cigarettes and lighter, stood up, descended the two steps that led to the beach, removed her shoes with a simple motion of her legs and feet, and headed towards the sea. When she reached the water's edge, she stopped, letting the sea caress her feet.

She hadn't told Montalbano to follow her. Just like that evening in Fiacca. And so the inspector remained seated at the table. Some ten minutes later, he saw her returning. Before ascending the two steps, she put her shoes back on.

When she sat down before him, Montalbano had the impression that the blue of her eyes was slightly brighter than usual. Rachele looked at him and smiled.

Then a tear that had remained half suspended fell from her left eye and rolled down her cheek.

"I think a grain of sand must have got in my eye," said Rachele, clearly fibbing.

The waiter returned like a nightmare.

"Has the lady decided?"

"What have you got?" asked Montalbano.

"We've got a mixed fish fry, grilled fish, swordfish however you like it, mullet *alla livornese* — "

"I only want a salad," said Rachele. Then, turning to the inspector: "Sorry, I just can't eat any more."

"No problem. I'll have a salad, too. However . . ."

"However?" said the waiter.

"Throw in some green and black olives, celery, carrots, capers, anything else the chef can think of."

"I'll have mine that way, too," declared Rachele.

"Would you like another bottle?"

There was enough left for two more glasses, one each.

"For me, that's enough," she said.

Montalbano gestured no, and the waiter left, perhaps mildly disappointed at the scantness of their order.

"I apologize for a few minutes ago," said Rachele. "I got up and walked away without saying anything. It's just that . . . I didn't want to start crying in front of you."

Montalbano didn't open his mouth.

"It happens to me sometimes," she continued, "but not very often, unfortunately."

"Why do you say 'unfortunately'?"

"You know, Salvo, it's very hard for me to cry when something bad or something sad happens. It all stays inside me. That's just the way I am."

"I saw you cry at the police station."

"That was only the second or third time in my life. Whereas — and this is what's so strange — I often weep uncontrollably in moments of . . . well, I wouldn't say happiness, that's too big a word. It would be more accurate to say that it's when I have a feeling of great calm inside me, when all the bumps are smoothed over, all the . . . But that's enough; I don't want to bore you with descriptions of my inner life."

This time, too, Montalbano said nothing.

But he was wondering how many Racheles there were inside Rachele.

The one he had met the first time at the station was an intelligent, rational woman, ironic and very much in control of herself. The one he had dealt with in Fiacca was a woman who had lucidly obtained what she wanted while managing, at the same time, to let go of herself completely in an instant, losing all lucidity and self-control. And the one who was sitting in front of him now was instead a vulnerable woman who had told him, without saying so directly, how unhappy she was, how rare were the moments of serenity in which she felt at peace with herself.

On the other hand, what on earth did he know about women?

Madamina, il catalogo è questo. And the list was a miserable one: one relationship before Livia; Livia; the twenty-year-old girl he didn't even want to name; and now Rachele.

And what about Ingrid? But Ingrid was a case apart. In their relationship, the line of demarcation between friendship and something else was really, really fine.

Of course, he'd met women, plenty of them, over the course of his many investigations, but these were all acquaintances made in very specific circumstances, in which the women all had a stake in presenting themselves as different from how they really were.

176

The waiter brought the salads. Which refreshed the tongue, the palate, and the mind.

"Would you like a whisky?"

"Why not?"

They ordered the drinks, which arrived at once. Now the moment had come to discuss the matter of most concern to Rachele.

"I brought a magazine with me, but I left it in the car," Montalbano began.

"What magazine?"

"The one featuring photos of Lo Duca's horses. I mentioned it to you over the phone."

"Oh, yes. And I think I told you that mine had a white spot shaped like a star on its flank. Poor Super!"

"How did you develop this passion for horses?"

"I got it from my father. I guess you don't know I was once champion of all Europe."

Montalbano's jaw dropped.

"Really?"

"Yes. I also twice won the Piazza di Siena competition, I've won in Madrid, and at Longchamps, too . . . Past glories."

There was a pause. Montalbano decided to lay his cards on the table.

"Why were you so insistent about seeing me?"

She gave a start, perhaps because of the directness of the attack, which she hadn't expected. Then she sat up straight, and Montalbano understood that he now had before him the same Rachele as the first time at the station.

"For two reasons. The first is strictly personal."

"Tell me."

"Since I don't think that, after I leave, we'll ever see each other again, I wanted to explain my behaviour the other night in Fiacca. So you won't have a distorted memory of me."

"There's no need for explanation," said Montalbano, suddenly feeling uncomfortable again.

"Yes there is. Ingrid, who knows me well, should have warned you that I . . . well . . . I don't quite know how to put it . . ."

"If you don't know how to say it, don't say it."

"If I like a man, I mean, if I really like a man, deep down, which doesn't happen to me very often, I can't help but . . . start things out with him in a way that for other women is the point of culmination. There. I don't know if I — "

"You've made yourself perfectly clear."

"Afterwards, two things can happen. Either I no longer want to hear even the slightest mention of him, or else I try, in every way possible, to keep him close to me, as a friend, or lover . . . And when I said I enjoyed you — and, incidentally, Ingrid told me you were upset about that — I wasn't thinking about what had just happened between us, but about what you are like, the way you act . . . in short, you as a man, taken all together. I realize my statement could be taken the wrong way. But I wasn't mistaken, since you're giving me the gift of an evening like this. End of discussion."

"And the second reason?"

"It's to do with the stolen horses. But I've thought it over again and I'm no longer sure there's any point in talking to you about it."

"Why not?"

"Because you said you're not handling the case. I don't want to tell you things that might just be a bother to you, on top of all the others you've already got."

"You can talk to me about it anyway, if you want."

"The other day I went with Chichi to the stables, and we ran into the vet, who was there to do his routine checkups."

"What is his name?"

"Mario Anzalone. He's very good."

"I don't know him. So what happened?"

"Well, when talking to Lo Duca, the vet said he didn't understand why the thieves took Rudy and not Moonbeam, the horse I rode in the race at Fiacca."

"Why?"

"He said that if there had been an expert among the thieves, he would surely have preferred Moonbeam to Rudy. In the first place, because Moonbeam was a far better horse than Rudy, and secondly, because it was clear that Rudy was ill and couldn't be easily cured. In fact, for this reason, he himself had suggested that we put him down, to spare him the suffering."

"And how did Lo Duca react? Did you notice?"

"Yes, I did. He replied that he was too fond of that horse."

"What was it ill with?"

"Viral arteritis. It creates lesions in the artery walls."

"So, it is as if the thieves had entered a luxury showroom and stolen one very expensive car and a broken-down Fiat 500."

"More or less, yes."

"Is the illness contagious?"

"Well, yes. In fact, during the ride back to Montelusa, I got upset at Chichi. 'What is this?' I said. 'You said you would be happy to lodge my horse, and you put him right next to a sick horse?'"

"Where did you keep him the other times you came here?"

"In Fiacca, with the Barone Piscopo."

"And how did Lo Duca defend himself?"

"He said that his horse's illness was already past the contagious stage. And he said that if I wanted — even though at this point it would have been completely pointless — I could phone the vet, who would surely confirm what he'd said."

"The horse, however, was dying."

"Right."

"So why bother to steal it?"

"That's why I wanted to see you. I asked myself the same thing, and came to a conclusion that contradicts what Chichi told you in Fiacca."

"Namely?"

"That they wanted to steal and kill only my horse, and that, since Rudy looked almost exactly like Super, they couldn't work out which one was mine, and so they took both. They wanted Chichi to look bad, and it worked."

180

This was a hypothesis they had already considered at the station.

"Did you read the newspaper yesterday?" Rachele continued.

"No."

"The *Corriere dell'Isola* devoted a great deal of space to the theft of the two horses. The reporters, however, seem not to know that mine was killed."

"How could they have known?"

"But everyone in Fiacca saw me ride a horse that wasn't mine! And surely some people would have asked some questions. Super was a horse who had won many important races; he was very well known in equestrian circles."

"Always ridden by you?"

Rachele laughed in her way.

"I wish!"

Then she stopped and asked:

"Tell me something. Have you ever actually witnessed a proper horse race, or a horse show?"

"Fiacca was the first time."

"Are you a football fan?"

"When the national team plays, I'll usually watch a few matches. But I prefer Formula One races, maybe because I've never been a very good driver."

"But Ingrid told me you swim a lot."

"Yes, but not for sport."

They finished their whiskies.

"Has Lo Duca inquired at Montelusa Central on the progress of the investigation?"

"Yes. They told him there were no new developments. And I fear there are not going to be any."

"You never know. Want another whisky?"

"No, thanks."

"What do you want to do?"

"If you don't mind, I'd like to go home."

"Feeling sleepy?"

"No. I just want to get into bed and curl up for a long time with my memories of this evening."

When it came time to say goodbye in the parking area of the Marinella Bar, they both very naturally embraced and kissed.

"Are you going to be staying much longer?"

"Another three days, at least. I'll give you a ring tomorrow to say goodbye. Is that all right?"

"Of course."

CHAPTER
FOURTEEN

When he opened his eyes, it was already broad daylight. But that morning he didn't feel like closing them immediately, in rejection of the day ahead. Perhaps because he'd had a good night's sleep, straight through from the moment he fell asleep to the moment he woke up, the rarest of things in recent times.

He remained in bed, watching the endlessly varying play of light and shadow that the sun's rays, passing through the slats in the blind, projected onto the ceiling. A man walking on the beach became a Giacometti-like figure, looking as if he were made of interwoven strands of yarn.

He remembered how as a little boy he could keep his eye glued for a whole hour to a kaleidoscope his uncle had bought for him, spellbound by the continually changing forms and colours. His uncle had also bought him a tin revolver, whose bullets were caps, dark red strips with little black dots that passed under the hammer and went *pop! pop!* when struck.

This memory called back to mind the shoot-out between Galluzzo and the men who'd tried to burn down his house.

It occurred to him how strange it was that those people, who wanted something from him but didn't say what, had let twenty-four hours pass without giving any more signs of themselves. And to think they were in such a hurry! How could they suddenly let go of the reins around his neck?

Upon asking himself this question, he started laughing, because never before would he have thought of such a thing in terms relating to horses.

Was this due to the case he was investigating, or was it because, deep down, the evening he'd spent with Rachele was still on his mind?

No doubt about it, Rachele was a woman who —

The phone rang.

Montalbano leapt out of bed, more to escape the thought of Rachele at once than out of any anxiousness to answer it.

It was six-thirty.

"Ahh Chief, Chief! Iss Catarella!"

The inspector felt like playing around.

"I'm sorry, what was that?" he said, altering his voice.

"Iss Catarella, Chief!"

"This is Fire Station Number 2373. If you want to speak with the fire chief, you'll have to call the fire department, during regular hours, of course."

"*O matre santa!* I mussa gotta wrong number. Beckin' y' pardon, sir."

He called right back.

"Hallo! Izz 'iss Fire Station 3723?"

"No, Cat. It's Montalbano. Wait just a second, while I look up the fire station's number for you."

"No no no, Chief, I don't want no fire station!"

"So why are you trying to phone them?"

"I donno. Sorry, Chief, I'm confused. Wanna hang up so's I can start all over again?"

"All right."

He rang a third time.

"Izzat choo, Chief?"

"It's me."

"Wha', was you asleep?"

"No, I was dancing the jitterbug."

"Rilly? You know how ado that?"

"Cat, just tell me what's up."

"They found a corpus."

How could you go wrong? If Catarella called at the crack of dawn, it always meant death in the morning.

"Male or female?"

"Iss o' the male persuasion."

"Where'd they find it?"

"In Spinoccia districk."

"Where's that?"

"Dunno, Chief. But Gallo's on 'is way."

"Where? To go look at the corpse?"

"No, Chief, sir, 'e's comin' a get you, poissonally in poisson. 'E's got a car an's gonna betake you to the premisses, which'd be in Spinoccia districk."

"But couldn't Augello go instead?"

"Nossir, in as far as atta moment when that I made 'im the tiliphone call, 'is wife said as how he was outta the house."

185

"But doesn't he have a mobile?"

"Yessir, 'e does. But iss ixtinguished."

Like Mimì's going to be out of the house at six in the morning! Obviously he was sleeping like a baby. And he'd told Beba to lie.

"And where's Fazio?"

"'E's already gone wit' Galluzzo to the beforementioned allocation."

When Gallo knocked at the door, the inspector had shaving cream all over his face.

"Come on in. I'll be ready in five minutes. Where the hell is this Spinoccia, anyway?"

"In heaven, Chief. Out in the country, about six miles before Giardina."

"Got any idea who was killed?"

"None, Chief. Fazio just phoned me and told me to come pick you up, so I came."

"But do you know how to get there?"

"In theory, yes. I had a look at a map."

"Look, Gallo, we're on an unmade road, not on the racetrack at Monza."

"I know, Chief. That's why I'm going slow."

Five minutes later:

"Gallo, I told you not to speed!"

"I'm going extremely slow, Chief."

To Gallo, going extremely slowly, on a stinking track full of potholes, crags, trenches, craters that looked like they'd been made by bombs, and dust galore, meant maintaining a speed of about fifty miles an hour.

186

They were passing through desolate country, parched and yellow, with a few rare, scraggly trees. It was a landscape Montalbano was quite fond of. They had already left the last little white cube of a house behind them, about a mile back. All they had run across were a little pushcart climbing up towards Giardina from Vigàta and a peasant with his mule, coming down in the opposite direction.

Rounding a bend, they saw the squad car in the distance and a donkey beside it. The ass, who was well aware that there was nothing to eat for miles around and just stood there, discouraged, looked at them with scant interest.

Gallo then launched the car off the road with a swerve so sudden that the inspector lurched sideways, despite the seat belt, and felt his head come detached from the rest of his body. He started cursing.

"Couldn't you stop the car a little further ahead?!"

"I'm stopping here to leave room for the other cars when they get here."

When they got out of the car, they noticed that beyond the squad car, on the left-hand side of the road, near a clump of sorghum, Fazio, Galluzzo, and a peasant were sitting on the ground, eating. The peasant had taken a loaf of wheat bread and a round of tumazzo cheese from his haversack and divided them up.

They made an idyllic, bucolic threesome, a sort of Sicilian *déjeuner sur l'herbe*.

Since the sun was already beating down hard, they were all in shirtsleeves.

As soon as Fazio and Galluzzo saw the inspector approaching, they stood up and put their jackets on. The peasant remained seated. But he brought a hand to his cap, giving a sort of military salute. He must have been at least eighty years old.

The dead man, wearing only a pair of underpants, was lying face down, parallel to the road. Clearly visible just under the left shoulder blade was one gunshot wound, with a little bit of blood around it. A chunk of flesh was missing from the right arm, the result of an animal bite. A hundred or so flies swarmed around the two wounds.

The inspector bent down to look at the bitten arm.

"'Zwas dogs," said the peasant, swallowing his last mouthful of bread and tumazzo. Then he extracted a bottle of wine from the haversack, pulled out the cork, sucked on it once, and put everything back.

"Did you find the body yourself?"

"Yessir. This mornin' when I's passin' by with my donkey," said the peasant, standing up.

"What's your name?"

"Giuseppe Contrera, n' my papers 're spotless."

He was keen to tell the cop that he had a clean record. But how had he been able to alert the police station from that desert? Carrier pigeon?

"Was it you who phoned us?"

"Nossir, my son."

"And where's your son?"

"At home, in Giardina."

"But was he with you when you discovered — "

"Nossir, he warn't. He was at his home. He was still asleep, the little gent. He's 'n accountant, you see."

"But if he wasn't with you — "

"May I, Chief?" asked Fazio, interrupting. "Our friend here, Contrera, called his son as soon as he discovered the body, and — "

"Yes, but *how* did he call him?"

"With this," said the peasant, pulling a mobile out of his pocket.

Montalbano balked. The peasant was dressed like an old-time peasant: fustian trousers, hobnail boots, collarless shirt, and waistcoat. The gadget seemed out of place in hands so callused they looked like a relief map of the Alps.

"So why didn't you call us directly yourself?"

"First of all," replied the peasant, "alls I know how to call with this thing is my son; an' seccunly, how's I sposta know your phone number?"

"The mobile," Fazio again explained, "was a gift from Signor Contrera's son, who's afraid that his father, given his age — "

"My boy Cosimo's a nitwit. 'N accountant an' a nitwit. He oughta worry 'bout his own hide an' not mine," the peasant declared.

"Did you get this man's name, address, and phone number?" Montalbano asked Fazio.

"Yeah, Chief."

"Then you can go now," Montalbano said to Contrera.

The peasant gave a military salute and mounted his donkey.

"Have you informed everyone?"

"Already done, Chief."

"Let's hope they arrive soon."

"Chief, it's gonna take another half hour at least, even if all goes well."

Montalbano made a snap decision.

"Gallo!"

"Your orders, Chief."

"How far are we from Giardina here?"

"By this road, I'd say fifteen minutes."

"Then let's go and have a cup of coffee. You two want me to bring you some?"

"No thanks," Fazio and Galluzzo replied in unison, with the flavour of the bread and tumazzo still in their mouths.

"I told you not to speed!"

"So who's speeding?"

And, indeed, after some ten minutes of bouncing along at fifty miles an hour, the car, just like that, ended up nose-first in a ditch as wide as the road itself, with the rear wheels practically spinning in air.

The manoeuvres to get unstuck — between heaving and ho-ing, cursing and shouting, with Gallo at the wheel one minute, Montalbano the next, shirts drenched with sweat — took a good half hour. On top of this, the left bumper had bent and was rubbing against the tyre. Gallo was finally forced to drive slowly.

In short, between one thing and another, by the time they got back to Spinoccia, over an hour had passed.

190

*   *   *

They were all there, except for Prosecutor Tommaseo. His absence worried Montalbano. It was anybody's guess when he might arrive, and he was liable to waste the inspector's whole morning. He drove worse than a blind man, crashing into every other tree he saw.

"Any news of Tommaseo?" Montalbano asked Fazio.

"Tommaseo's already gone!"

What, had he become Fangio on the Carrera Panamericana?

"Luckily he hitched a lift up with Dr Pasquano," Fazio continued. "He gave the go-ahead for the body to be removed, and got a lift back to Montelusa from Galluzzo."

When forensics had finished shooting their first series of photos, Pasquano had the body turned over. The victim must have been about fifty, perhaps slightly less. On his chest there was no exit wound from the bullet that had killed him.

"You know him?" the inspector asked Fazio.

"No."

Dr Pasquano finished examining the body, cursing the flies buzzing back and forth between the corpse and his face.

"What can you tell me, Doctor?"

Pasquano pretended not to have heard him. Montalbano repeated the question, pretending in turn that the doctor hadn't heard him. Then Pasquano gave Montalbano a dirty look, removing his gloves. He was all sweaty and red in the face.

"What can I tell you? It's a beautiful day."

191

"Gorgeous, isn't it? What can you tell me about the dead man?"

"You're a bigger pain in the arse than these flies, you know that? What the hell do you want me to tell you?"

He must have lost at poker the night before, at the club. Montalbano summoned his patience and dug in.

"Tell you what, Doctor. While you're talking, I'll wipe away your sweat, chase away the flies, and every so often kiss your forehead."

Pasquano started laughing. Then, in a single breath, he said:

"He was killed by a single shot to the shoulder. And you didn't need me to tell you that. The bullet did not exit the body. And you didn't need me to tell you that, either. He wasn't shot at this location because — and you can figure this out all by yourself, too — a man doesn't go walking outside in his underpants, not even on a shitty track like this one. He's probably been dead — and this, too, you have enough experience to figure out for yourself — for at least twenty-four hours. As for the bite on his arm, any idiot can see that it was a dog. To conclude, there was no need for you to force me to speak, making me waste my breath and busting my balls to hell and back. Have I made myself clear?"

"Perfectly."

"And a good day to one and all."

He turned his back, got in his car, and drove away.

Vanni Arquà, chief of forensics, kept having his men waste roll after roll of film for no reason. Of the thousands of shots taken, only two or three would prove important. Fed up, the inspector decided to go back to town. After all, what was he doing there?

"I'm leaving," he said to Fazio. "I'll see you at the station. Gallo, come on, can we go?"

He said nothing to Arquà, who, for his part, hadn't greeted him upon arriving. You certainly couldn't say they were fond of each other.

In the effort he had made to pull the car out of the ditch, the dust had not only soiled his clothes, it had filtered through his shirt, and the sweat made it stick to his skin.

He didn't feel like spending the day at the station in that condition. It was, moreover, almost noon.

"Take me to Marinella," he said to Gallo.

Opening the front door, he realized at once that Adelina had finished her work and gone.

He went straight into the bathroom, got undressed, took a shower, threw the dirty clothes into the hamper, then went into the bedroom and opened the cupboard to find a clean suit. He noticed that one of the pairs of trousers was still in the plastic dry-cleaners' bag; apparently Adelina had picked them up that same morning. He decided to wear them with a jacket he liked, and to break in one of the shirts he had just bought.

Then he got back into the car and drove to Enzo's trattoria.

Since it was still early, there was only one other customer. The television was reporting that the body of an unknown man had been found by a fisherman in a reed bed in the district of Spinoccia. Police had ruled his death a crime, as clear signs of strangulation had been detected around the man's neck. It also appeared, though had not yet been confirmed, that the killer had ferociously bitten the corpse all over. The case was being investigated by Chief Inspector Salvo Montalbano. More details on the next newscast.

And so, this time, too, the television had done his job for him, which was to convey information dressed up in details and circumstances that were either completely wrong, utterly false, or pure fantasy. And yet the public swallowed it all. Why did the TV people do it? To make an already horrifying crime as hair-raising as possible? It was no longer enough to report a death; they had to provoke horror. After all, hadn't the United States unleashed a war based on lies, stupidities, and mystifications that the most important figures in the country swore to by all that was holy in front of the whole world's television cameras? After which, those same television cameras, and the people behind them, on their own, put the icing on the cake. And by the way, that anthrax case, whatever became of that? How was it that, from one day to the next, everybody stopped talking about it?

"Excuse me, but, if the other customer doesn't mind, could you please turn off the television?"

Enzo went over to the other diner, who, turning towards the inspector, declared:

"Yeah, you can turn it off. I don't give a shit about that stuff."

194

Fat and about fifty, the man was eating a triple serving of spaghetti with clam sauce.

The inspector ate the same thing. Followed by the usual mullets.

When he came out of the trattoria, he decided there was no need for a stroll along the jetty, and so returned to the office, where he had a mountain of papers to sign.

By the time he had finished most of his bureaucratic chores, it was already well past five o'clock. He decided to do the rest the following day. As he was setting down his ballpoint, the telephone rang. Montalbano looked at it with suspicion. For some time now, he was becoming more and more convinced that all telephones were endowed with an autonomous, thinking brain. There was no other way to explain the fact that they were ringing with increasing frequency at either the most opportune or the most inopportune moments, and never at moments when you weren't doing anything.

"Ahh, Chief, Chief! That'd be the lady Esther Mann. Do I put 'er true?"

"Yes . . . Hello, Rachele. How are you doing?"

"Great. And you?"

"Me too. Where are you?"

"In Montelusa. But I'm about to leave."

"You're going back to Rome? But you said — "

"No, Salvo, I'm just going to Fiacca."

The sudden pang of jealousy he felt was unwarranted. Worse than that, it was totally unjustified. There was no reason in the world for him to feel that way.

"I'm going with Ingrid, to attend to some business."

"Do you have business interests in Fiacca?"

"No. I meant sentimental business."

And this could mean only one thing: that she was going there to give Guido his marching papers.

"But we'll be back this evening. Shall we get together tomorrow?"

"Let's try."

CHAPTER
FIFTEEN

Barely five minutes later, the telephone rang again.

"Ahh, Chief! 'At'd be Dr Pisquano."

"On the line?"

"Yessir."

"Put 'im on."

"How is it you haven't busted my balls yet today?" Pasquano began, with the courtesy for which he was famous.

"Why should I have done that?"

"To find out the results of the post-mortem."

"Whose?"

"Montalbano, this is a clear sign of old age. A sign that your brain cells are disintegrating with increasing speed. The first symptom is memory loss. Did you know that? For example, does it sometimes happen that you'll do something one minute, and the next minute you'll forget that you did it?"

"No. But aren't you five years older than me, Doctor?"

"Yes, but the actual age doesn't mean anything. There are people who are already old at twenty. In any case, I think it's clear to all concerned that you're the more doddering of the two of us."

"Thanks. You want to tell me what post-mortem you're talking about?"

"This morning's corpse."

"Oh, no, you don't, Doctor! The last thing I might imagine was that you would perform that post-mortem so soon! What, were you good friends with the dead man or something? Normally you let days and days go by before — "

"This time I happened to have two free hours before lunch, and so I got him out of my hair. It turns out there are two minor new developments, with respect to what I told you this morning. The first is that I've recovered the bullet and sent it at once to forensics, who, naturally, won't have any news on it until after the next presidential election."

"But the last one was barely three months ago!"

"Precisely."

It was true. He recalled that he'd sent them the iron bars used to kill the horse for fingerprints, but still hadn't heard back from them.

"And what's the second development?"

"I found some traces of cotton wool inside the wound."

"What does that mean?"

"It means that the person who shot him is not the same as the one who dumped him by the roadside."

"Care to elaborate on that a little?"

"Gladly, especially considering the age of the person involved."

"Whose age?"

"Why, yours, of course. That's another product of ageing: increasingly slow to comprehend."

"Doctor, why don't you go get — "

"I wish! It might improve my luck at poker! Anyway, I was explaining that, in my opinion, someone shot the soon-to-be dead man, gravely injuring him. Then a friend, or an accomplice, or somebody, took him home and tried to staunch the blood flowing out of the wound. But the victim must have died shortly thereafter. So the helper waited until dark and then loaded the body into his car and dumped it in the open countryside, as far as possible from his house."

"It's a plausible hypothesis."

"Thanks for understanding without need of further explanation."

"Listen, Doctor. Any distinguishing marks?"

"Appendectomy scar."

"That should help in the identification."

"The identification of whom?"

"The dead man, who else?"

"The dead man never had an appendectomy!"

"But you just said he did!"

"You see, my friend? That's another sign of ageing. You asked me the question in such a confused way that I thought you were asking me if *I* had any distinguishing marks."

Pasquano was just pulling Montalbano's leg. That was how he got his fun.

"All right, Doctor, now that we've cleared up that misunderstanding, I will repeat my question, as straightforwardly as possible, so that it won't require too much mental effort on your part, which could be fatal. Did the dead body on which you performed the post-mortem today have any distinguishing marks?"

"I'd say it most certainly did."

"Could you please tell me what those are?"

"No. It's something I'd rather put in writing."

"But when will I get your report?"

"When I have the time and the desire to write it."

And there was no way to persuade him otherwise.

The inspector stayed a little while longer in his office, and then, as there was still no sign or word from either Fazio or Augello, he went home.

Shortly before he was about to go to bed, Livia phoned. This time, too, things did not go well. The conversation did not end in a squabble, but just barely missed.

Words were no longer enough to help them get along and understand each other. It was as if their words, if you looked them up in the dictionary, had different and opposite definitions depending on whether he or Livia was using them. And these double meanings were a continual cause of confusion, misunderstandings, and quarrels.

But if they got together and were able to remain silent, one beside the other, things completely changed. It was as if their bodies started first to sniff each other, to pick up the other's scent from a distance, then to speak to one another, with complete understanding, in a wordless language made up of small signs such as a leg moving an inch or two to get closer to the other, or a head leaning ever so slightly towards the other head. And, inevitably, the two bodies, still silent, would end up in a desperate embrace.

He slept poorly and was even startled awake by a nightmare in the middle of the night. How was it possible that he had gone years and years without even the slightest thought about horses and horse racing, and now he was actually dreaming about them?

He found himself in a racetrack with three tracks running parallel to one another. With him was Commissioner Bonetti-Alderighi, impeccably dressed in riding clothes. For his part, Montalbano was unshaven and dishevelled, in a shabby suit with one torn sleeve. He looked like a beggar on the street. The grandstand was packed full of people shouting and gesticulating.

"Augello, put on your glasses before mounting!" Bonetti-Alderighi commanded him.

"I'm not Augello. I'm Montalbano."

"It makes no difference, put them on just the same! Can't you see you're blind as a bat?"

"I can't put 'em on, I lost 'em onna way 'ere, I got holes in m' pockets," he replied, feeling ashamed.

"Penalty! You spoke in dialect!" shouted a voice, as if from a loudspeaker.

"You see the trouble you're getting me in?" the commissioner reproached him.

"I'm sorry."

"Get the horse!"

He turned to grab the horse, but realized it was made of bronze and half collapsed, sitting on its haunches, just like the RAI horse.

"How can I?"

"Grab it by the mane!"

The instant his hand touched the mane, the horse thrust its head between the inspector's legs, hoisted him up on its neck, and raised its head, making him slide down the neck, so that he ended up mounted, but backwards, facing its haunches.

He heard laughter from the grandstand. Feeling insulted, with great effort he turned around, grabbing the mane as hard as he could, because the horse, having now become flesh and blood, was not saddled and had no reins.

Someone fired some sort of cannon, and the horse set off at a gallop towards the middle track between the other two.

"No! No!" Bonetti-Alderighi yelled.

"No! No!" the people in the grandstand repeated.

"You're on the wrong track," Bonetti-Alderighi yelled.

Everyone was gesturing, but he couldn't make out the gestures and saw only blurry splotches of colour, since he had lost his glasses. He realized the horse was doing something wrong, but how do you tell a horse it's doing something wrong? And why wasn't it the right track?

He understood why a moment later, when the animal began to walk with great effort. The track was made of sand, the same kind of sand as on a beach. But very fine and deep, so that the horse's hooves sank further into it with each step until they were completely submerged. A track of sand. Why did this have to happen to him, of all people? He tried to turn the

202

animal's head to the left, so that it would take the other track. But he suddenly realized that the other, parallel tracks were gone; the racetrack with its fences and grandstand had vanished, and even the track he was on was no longer there, because it had all become an ocean of sand.

Now, with each laboured step it took, the animal sank further and further, first with its legs, then its belly, then even its chest submerged in sand. At some point he no longer felt it moving beneath him. It had been suffocated by the sand.

He tried to climb down, but the sand kept him imprisoned. He realized he was going to die in that desert. As he started to cry, a man materialized a few steps away from him, but he couldn't make out his face, again because he didn't have his glasses.

"You know the way out of this situation," the man said to him.

He wanted to answer him, but as soon as he opened his mouth, the sand came pouring in, threatening to suffocate him.

In a desperate attempt to draw a breath, he woke up.

He had dreamt a sort of mishmash of fantasy and things that had actually happened to him. But what did it mean that he was running on the wrong track?

He got to his office later than usual, because he'd had to stop at the bank after finding a letter in his letter box threatening to cut off his electricity for failure to pay the last bill. Yet he had arranged for the bank to pay the bills! He stood in line for almost an hour, showed the letter to a clerk, who began looking things up. It turned out that the bill had been paid on time.

"There must have been a mistake, sir."

"And what am I supposed to do?"

"Don't worry, sir, we'll take care of it."

For a long time he had been thinking about rewriting the Constitution. Since everybody and his dog was doing it, why couldn't he? Article One would begin as follows: "Italy is a precarious republic founded on mistakes."

"Ahh Chief, Chief! F'rensics jist now sint us this invilope!"

The inspector opened it on his way to his room.

It contained a few photographs of the man found dead in Spinoccia, with related information as to age, height, colour of eyes, etc . . . There was no mention of distinguishing marks.

There was no point in passing the photos on to Catarella and asking him to search the missing persons files for faces that might match. He was putting them back into the envelope when Mimì Augello came in. He took them back out and handed them to his second-in-command.

"Have you ever seen him?"

"Is that the dead man from Spinoccia?"

"Yes."

Mimì put on his glasses. Montalbano squirmed uneasily in his chair.

"Never seen him before," said Augello, laying the photos and envelope on the desk and putting the glasses back in his shirt pocket.

"Could I try them?"

"Try what?"

"The glasses."

Augello handed them to him. Montalbano put them on, and everything suddenly looked like a blurry photograph. He took them off and gave them back to Mimì.

"I can see better with my father's pair."

"But you can't ask everyone you meet with glasses if you can try them on! You simply have to go and see an optician! He'll examine you and prescribe — "

"OK, OK. I'll go one of these days. Tell me, how is it I didn't see you all day yesterday?"

"I spent the whole morning and afternoon looking into the business of that little boy, Angelo Verruso. Remember?"

A little boy not six years old, returning home from school, had started crying and refused to eat. Finally, after much insistence, his mother had succeeded in getting him to tell her that his teacher had forced him into a cupboard and made him do "dirty things". When the mother asked for details, he said the teacher had taken his thingy out and made him touch it. A sensible woman, Mrs Verruso did not believe that the teacher, a family man of about fifty, was capable of such behaviour; on the other hand, neither did she want to disbelieve her son.

Since she was a friend of Beba, she spoke to her about it. And Beba, in turn, talked to her husband, Mimì, about it. Who then related the whole matter to Montalbano.

"How'd it go?"

"Listen, we're better off dealing with criminals than with these little kids. It's impossible to tell when they're telling the truth and when they're lying. And I also have to proceed with caution; I don't want to destroy the teacher. All it takes is for a rumour to start circulating, and he's ruined . . ."

"But what was your impression?"

"That the teacher didn't do anything. I didn't hear a single bad thing about him. Anyway, the cupboard in question is barely big enough to hold a bucket and two brooms."

"So why would the kid make up a story like that?"

"In my opinion, to get back at the teacher, who he thinks is mean to him."

"Deliberately?"

"Are you kidding? Want to know what Angelo's latest exploit was? He shat on a newspaper, folded it up into a little package, and slipped it into one of the drawers in the teacher's desk."

"So why did they name him Angelo?"

"When he was born, the parents obviously had no idea how the little imp would turn out."

"Is he still going to school?"

"No, I advised the mother to report him ill."

"Good idea."

"Good morning, Inspectors," said Fazio, coming in. He saw the photos of the dead man.

"Can I take one of these?" he asked. "I'd like to show it around."

"Go ahead. What did you do yesterday afternoon?"

"I kept asking around about Gurreri."

"Did you talk to his wife?"

"Not yet. I'll be going later today."

"What did you find out?"

"Chief, what Lo Duca told you is true, at least in part."

"What part?"

"That Gurreri left his home over three months ago. All the neighbours heard him."

"Heard what?"

"Heard him yelling at his wife, calling her a whore and a slut, and saying he was never coming back."

"Did he say he wanted to take revenge on Lo Duca?"

"No, they didn't hear him say that. But they also can't swear he didn't say it."

"Did the neighbour lady tell you anything else?"

"No, the neighbour lady didn't, but Don Minicuzzu did."

"And who is Don Minicuzzu?"

"A man who sells fruits and vegetables directly in front of where Gurreri lives and can see who goes in and out of the building."

"And what did he tell you?"

"Chief, according to Minicuzzu, Licco has never set foot in that building. So how could he be Gurreri's wife's lover?"

"But does he know Licco well?"

"Does he know him well? Licco's the one he used to pay the racket money to! And he told me something important, as well. One night he was worried he hadn't properly locked the metal shutter. So he got out of bed and went outside to check. When he was in front of his shop, the door to Gurreri's building opened, and out came Ciccio Bellavia, whom he knows well."

Imagine Ciccio Bellavia *not* crawling out of the sewer in this affair!

"And when was this?"

"Over three months ago."

"So our hypothesis is correct. Bellavia goes to Gurreri and offers him a deal. If his wife provides Licco with an alibi, saying she's his mistress, Gurreri gets taken on as a permanent member of the Cuffaros. Gurreri thinks it over a bit and then accepts, putting on the show about leaving home forever because his wife is cheating on him."

"You've got to admit, it's a pretty good scheme," Mimì commented. "But is Minicuzzu willing to testify?"

"Not on your life," said Fazio.

"So we're left with nothing," said Augello.

"There is one thing, however, that we should explore further," said Montalbano.

"What's that?"

"We know nothing about Gurreri's wife. Did she immediately go along because they offered her money? Or was she threatened? And how would she react to the possibility of ending up in jail for perjury? Does she know she's running that risk?"

"Chief," said Fazio, "if you ask me, Concetta Siragusa is an honest woman who had the bad luck to marry a crook. I haven't heard any malicious gossip about her conduct. I am sure they forced her to play along. Between her husband's slaps, punches, and kicks and whatever Ciccio Bellavia told her, the poor thing probably had no choice but to accept."

"You know what I say, Fazio? Maybe we're lucky you haven't talked to her yet."

"Why?"

"Because we need to think of a way to trip her up."

"I could go and talk to her," said Mimì.

"And what would you say to her?"

"That I'm a lawyer sent by the Cuffaros to instruct her as to what she should say at the trial. That way, as we're talking . . ."

"Mimì, what if they've already sent their lawyer, and she gets suspicious?"

"Yeah, you're right. Well, then, let's send her an anonymous letter."

"I'm sure she doesn't know how to read or write," said Fazio.

"I've got it!" Mimì persisted. "I'll dress up as a priest and — "

"You want to stop talking crap, Mimì? For the moment, nobody is going to go and talk to Concetta Siragusa. We'll think it over a bit, and when one of us has a good idea . . . We're not in such a hurry."

"I thought priest was a good idea," said Mimì.

The telephone rang.

"Ahh, Chief, Chief! Ahh, Chief, Chief!"

Four chiefs? It must be the commissioner.

"Is it the commissioner?"

"Yessir, Chief."

"Put him on," he said, turning on the speakerphone.

"Montalbano?"

"Good morning, Mr Commissioner, what can I do for you?"

"Could you come to my office right now? I'm sorry to disturb you, but it's something very serious, and I don't want to talk about it over the phone."

The tone of the commissioner's voice made him consent at once.

He hung up, and they all looked at one another.

"If he's talking like that, it really must be something serious," said Mimì.

CHAPTER
SIXTEEN

In the commissioner's waiting room, he inevitably ran
into Dr Lattes, the priest-like, unctuous cabinet chief.
But why was the guy always fiddling about in the
waiting room? Did he have too much time on his
hands? Didn't he have an office of his own? Couldn't
he go and scratch his balls behind his own desk? The
mere sight of him put Montalbano on edge. Upon
spotting the inspector, Lattes's face lit up as if he'd just
found out he won a few billion in the lottery.

"Ah, what a pleasure! What a joy! How are you, dear
Inspector?"

"Fine, thanks."

"And the missus?"

"She's getting by."

"And the children?"

"Growing, with thanks to the Madonna."

"Let us always give thanks."

Lattes was stuck on this idea that Montalbano was
married with at least two children. After a hundred or
so vain attempts to explain that he was a bachelor, the
inspector had given up. The phrase "with thanks to the
Madonna" was also *de rigueur* with Lattes.

"The commissioner asked me to — "

"Just knock and go in. He's waiting for you."

He rapped and entered.

But he froze for a moment in the doorway, taken aback to see Vanni Arquà seated in front of the commissioner's desk. What the hell was the chief of forensics doing there? Was he going to take part in this meeting, too? Why? In a twinkling, his antipathy towards Arquà shot up to maximum.

"Please come in, close the door, and sit down."

On other occasions, Bonetti-Alderighi had purposely made him stand. So that he could appreciate the distance between him, the commissioner, and a lowly chief inspector of a small-town police department. This time, however, the commissioner behaved differently. Indeed, just as Montalbano was about to sit down, his boss actually stood up and held out his hand. The inspector was literally scared. What could have happened for the commissioner to treat him so politely, like a normal person? Was he about to read him his death sentence?

Montalbano and Arquà greeted each other with a slight nod. Given their relationship, this was a major thaw.

"Montalbano, I wanted to see you because we have a rather delicate matter on our hands, and it has me very worried."

"I'm listening, Mr Commissioner."

"All right. As you already know, perhaps, Dr Pasquano has performed the post-mortem on the body found in Spinoccia."

"Yes, I know. But I haven't yet read the re —"

212

"I've requested it, actually, and shall have it this afternoon. But that's not the matter. The fact is that Dr Pasquano, with admirable speed, has already sent the bullet he extracted to the forensics lab."

"He told me that, too."

"Good. Well, when examining it, Dr Arquà, to his great surprise, found . . . but perhaps it's better if I let him tell you."

Vanni Arquà, however, did not open his mouth. He merely extracted a sealed cellophane packet from his pocket and handed it to the inspector. The bullet inside was quite visible; rather misshapen, but basically whole.

Montalbano found nothing strange about it.

"So?"

"It's a calibre-nine Parabellum," said Arquà.

"I could see that myself," said Montalbano, slightly resentful. "So what?"

"It's a calibre exclusive to our equipment," said Arquà.

"No, allow me to correct you. It is not exclusive to police equipment. It also happens to be the calibre used by the carabinieri, the finance police, the armed forces — "

"All right, all right," the commissioner interrupted him.

But the inspector pretended not to hear him:

"— and also all the crooks, and there are many of them — indeed the majority, I'd say — who have managed in one way or another to get their hands on military-grade weapons."

"I am very well aware of that," said Arquà, with a little smile that invited a pummelling.

"So what is the problem?"

"Let us proceed in orderly fashion, Montalbano," said the commissioner. "What you say is absolutely right, but we must absolutely clear the air of any possible suspicion."

"Suspicion of what?"

"That it might be one of our men who killed him. Do you know of any exchange of gunfire that took place during the day last Monday?"

"Not that I'm aware of . . ."

"That's what I was afraid of. This complicates matters," said the commissioner.

"Why?"

"Because if a journalist gets wind of this, can you imagine all the suspicions, insinuations, all the mud they'll hurl at us?"

"Well, let's not let them find out."

"It's not so simple. And if it turns out that this man was killed by one of ours for, let's say, personal reasons, I want to know. It really upsets me, it chagrins me, it disgusts me to think that there might be a killer among us."

At this point Montalbano rebelled.

"I understand how you feel, Mr Commissioner. But could you please tell me why I alone have been summoned to your office? Do you think perhaps that if there is a killer among us, he must be necessarily from my force and not from somewhere else?"

214

"It's because the body was found in an area between Vigàta and Giardina, and both Vigàta and Giardina are territorially part of your jurisdiction," said Arquà. "It is therefore logical to presume that — "

"It's not the least bit logical! That body could easily have been brought there from Fiacca, from Fela, from Gallotta, from Montelusa — "

"There's no need to get upset, Montalbano," the commissioner intervened. "What you say is absolutely true. But we've got to start somewhere, haven't we?"

"But why are you so fu — so stuck on this idea that it was someone from the police who did it?"

"That's not my idea at all," said the commissioner. "My goal is to prove incontrovertibly that it was not a member of the police who killed that man. And before the malicious rumours start circulating."

He was right, no doubt about it.

"That's going to take a while, you know."

"No matter. We'll take all the time we need; nobody's coming after us," said Bonetti-Alderighi.

"So how should I proceed?"

"You, in the meantime, should check, as discreetly as possible, to see if any cartridges are missing from the pistols used by the men in your department."

At that exact moment, without a sound, the ground beneath Montalbano's feet suddenly opened up, and he plummeted inside, chair and all. He had just remembered something. He managed, however, not to move, not to sweat, not to turn pale. He even managed, through an effort that cost him a year of his life, to smile faintly.

"Why are you smiling?"

"Because on Monday morning Corporal Galluzzo fired two shots at a dog that attacked me. Galluzzo had driven me home to Marinella, and the moment I got out of the car, this dog . . . Sergeant Fazio was also there."

"Did he kill it?" Arquà enquired.

"I don't understand the question."

"If he killed the animal, we'll try to track it down, remove the bullet, and we'll know — "

"What do you mean, 'if'? Are you trying to say my men don't know how to shoot?"

"Answer me, Montalbano," the commissioner intervened. "Did he hit the dog or not?"

"No, he missed it, and couldn't get off any more shots because the weapon jammed."

"Could I have it?" Arquà asked icily.

"Have what?"

"The weapon."

"Why?"

"I'd like to make a comparison."

If Arquà made his comparison by firing a shot from that pistol, they were all fucked — him, Galluzzo, and Fazio. He had to prevent this, at all costs.

"Ask the weapons department for it. I think they've still got it," said Montalbano.

Then he stood up, pale, hands shaking, nostrils flaring, and eyes flashing, and said in a voice cracking with rage:

"Mr Commissioner, Dr Arquà has deeply offended me!"

216

"Come now, Montalbano!"

"Oh, yes, sir, deeply offended me! And you are a witness, Mr Commissioner! And I shall ask you to testify! With his request, Dr Arquà has cast my words into doubt. The gun is at his disposal; but now he, Dr Arquà, must put himself, in turn, at my disposal."

Arquà seemed to fear he was actually being challenged to a duel.

"But I didn't mean . . ." he began.

"Come now, Montalbano . . ." Bonetti-Alderighi repeated.

Montalbano clenched his fists, turning them white.

"No, Mr Commissioner, I am sorry. I maintain that I have been gravely offended. I shall conduct every examination you have ordered me to do. But if Dr Arquà requests my corporal's weapon, I will submit my resignation forthwith. With all the ensuing publicity. Good day."

And before Bonetti-Alderighi had time to reply, the inspector turned his back on the two men, opened the door, and left, congratulating himself on the resounding success of the tragic scene he had just staged. He could certainly have had a career in Hollywood.

He needed to confirm something at once. He got in his car and went straight to Pasquano's office.

"Is the doctor in?"

"He's in, but . . ."

"No problem, I'll see him myself."

There were two round windows in the door of the room in which Pasquano worked.

The inspector had a look before going inside. Pasquano was washing his hands, but still wearing his blood-stained apron. The table on which he performed his post-mortems was empty. Montalbano pushed the door open. Seeing him, the doctor started cursing.

"Holy fucking Christ! Can't I get away from you even here? Just lay yourself down on this table, I'll take care of you in a jiffy."

He grabbed some sort of bone-cutting saw. Montalbano took a few steps back. With Pasquano it was always best to be careful.

"Just answer yes or no, Doc, and I'll be on my way."

"Do you swear?"

"I swear. Did the skull of the body from Spinoccia show any signs of having been drilled or something similar?"

"Yes," said Pasquano.

"Thanks," said the inspector.

And he ran away. He had the confirmation he wanted.

"Ahh, Chief! I wannata report 'at — "

"You can tell me later. Get me Fazio at once and don't put any calls through to me! I'm not here for anyone!"

Fazio came running.

"What's up, Chief?"

"Come in, shut the door, and take a seat."

"I'm all ears, Chief."

"I know who the dead man from Spinoccia is."

"Really?!"

218

"Gurreri. And I also know who killed him."

"Who?"

"Galluzzo."

"Fuck!"

"Exactly."

"So the body's Gurreri's? That would make him one of the two guys who tried to set your house on fire on Monday."

"Right."

"But are you sure?"

"Absolutely. Dr Pasquano told me he found signs of the operation that was performed on Gurreri's head three years ago."

"But who told you the dead man might be Gurreri?"

"Nobody told me. I had an intuition."

He told Fazio about his meeting with the commissioner and Arquà.

"This means we're in deep shit, Chief."

"No. The shit's there, and we're close, but we're not in it yet."

"But if Dr Arquà insists on seeing that gun — "

"I don't think he will. In fact I'm sure the commissioner will tell him to drop it. I made a terrible scene. However . . . Excuse me, but the weapons that need adjusting, we send them to Montelusa, right?"

"Yes, sir."

"And has weapons sent Galluzzo's gun to be fixed yet?"

"No, not yet. But I only found out by chance this morning. I wanted to give them Patrolman Ferrara's gun, too, which also jammed, but since neither

219

Turturici nor Manzella were there, and they're in charge of —"

"That little shit Arquà won't have to ask me for the weapon. Since I said Galluzzo's gun jammed, he's going to check every pistol that comes in from our station. We absolutely need to screw him before he screws us."

"How are we going to do that?"

"I just had an idea. Have you still got Ferrara's pistol?"

"Yes, sir."

"Wait. I need to make a phone call."

He raised the receiver.

"Catarella? Please call the c'mishner, then put him through to me."

The call went through at once. He turned on the speakerphone.

"What can I do for you, Montalbano?"

"Mr Commissioner, I'd like to say first of all that I feel deeply mortified for letting myself get carried away in your presence, with a terrible, nervous outburst that — "

"Well, I'm pleased that you — "

"I also wanted to inform you that I'll be sending Dr Arquà the weapon in question" — *weapon in question* wasn't bad — "without delay, for any verifications or tests he deems necessary. And I beg you again, Mr Commissioner, to forgive me and accept my deepest, humblest — "

"Apologies accepted. I am glad it's all turned out for the better between you and Arquà. Goodbye, Montalbano."

"My very best wishes, Mr Commissioner."

He hung up.

"What on earth are you up to?" asked Fazio.

"Go and get Ferrara's weapon, remove two cartridges from the clip, and hide them well. We'll need them later. Then put it in a box all nicely wrapped up as a present and take it to Dr Arquà with my compliments."

"And what do I tell Ferrara? If he doesn't hand in his jammed pistol, they won't give him another."

"Get weapons to give you back Galluzzo's, too. Tell them I need it. Work out a way to tell them that you also gave me Ferrara's gun, so they can give you a replacement for him. If Manzella and Turturici ask me to explain, I'll say I want to bring them to Montelusa myself to protest. The key is to let three or four days pass."

"So how do we deal with Galluzzo?"

"If he's here, send him in."

Five minutes later, Galluzzo appeared.

"You wanted me, Chief?"

"Sit down, killer."

When he had finished talking to Galluzzo, he looked at his watch and realized he had taken too long. At that hour, Enzo the restaurateur had already lowered the metal shutter.

So he decided to make his last remaining move now, without wasting any more time. He took a photo of Gurreri, put it in his pocket, went out, got in his car, and drove off.

Via Nicotera was not really a street, properly speaking, but a long, narrow alleyway in Piano Lanterna, the elevated part of town. Number 38 was a dilapidated little two-storey building with a locked front door. Opposite it was a greengrocer's shop that must have been Don Minicuzzu's. Given the hour, however, it was closed. The little building had an intercom system. He pressed the button next to the name Gurreri. A moment later the door clicked open, without anyone having asked who was ringing.

There was no lift, but the house, after all, was small. There were two apartments on each floor. Gurreri lived on the top floor. The front door was open.

"May I?" he asked.

"Please come in," said a woman's voice.

A tiny little vestibule with two doors, one leading to the dining room, the other to the bedroom. At once Montalbano smelled the odour of heart-breaking poverty. A woman of about thirty, shabby and dishevelled, was waiting for him in the dining room. She must have married Gurreri when still a very young girl, and she must have been beautiful, since, in spite of everything, something of her lost beauty still remained in her face and body.

"Whattya want?" she asked.

Montalbano could see the fear in her eyes.

"I'm a police inspector, Mrs Gurreri. My name is Montalbano."

"I a'ready tol' everything to the carabinieri."

"I know, signora. Why don't we sit down?"

They sat down. She on the edge of her chair, tense, ready to run away.

"I know you've been called upon to testify at the Licco trial."

"Yessir."

"But that's not why I came here."

She immediately seemed a bit relieved. But the fear remained deep in her eyes.

"So whattya want?"

Montalbano found himself at a crossroads. He didn't feel like being brutal with her; he felt too sorry for her. Now that she was sitting there before him, he was positive the young woman had been persuaded to become Licco's mistress not by money, but by beatings and threats.

On the other hand, it was possible he wouldn't get anywhere with kindness and moderation. Perhaps the best thing was to shock her.

"How long has it been since you last saw your husband?"

"Three months, give or take a few days."

"And you haven't heard from him since?"

"No, sir."

"You don't have any children, do you?"

"No, sir."

"Do you know someone by the name of Ciccio Bellavia?"

The fear returned, animal-like, to her eyes. Montalbano noticed that her hands were trembling slightly.

"Yes, sir."

"Has he come here?"

"Yes, sir."

"How many times?"

"Twice. Both times with my husband."

"I think you should come with me, signora."

"Now?"

"Now."

"Where to?"

"To the morgue."

"Whass that?"

"It's where they put dead people."

"Why should I go there?"

"We need you to make an identification."

He took the photograph out of his pocket.

"Is this your husband?"

"Yes, sir. When'd they take this? Why do I have to come? . . ."

"Because we're convinced that Ciccio Bellavia killed your husband."

She bolted upright. Then she staggered, her body swaying back and forth, and grabbed the table.

"Damn him! Damn that Bellavia! He swore to me he wouldn't do nothin' to him!"

She couldn't go on. Her legs buckled and she fell to the floor, unconscious.

CHAPTER
SEVENTEEN

"Look, I haven't got much time. And don't get into the bad habit of dropping in without an appointment," said Prosecutor Giarrizzo.

"You're right, sir. I'm sorry to barge in like this."

"You've got five minutes. Speak."

Montalbano glanced at his watch.

"I've come to give you the second episode of the adventures of Inspector Martinez. I think you'll find it quite interesting."

Giarrizzo looked baffled.

"And who is this Martinez?"

"Have you forgotten? Don't you remember the hypothetical police inspector you spoke to me about hypothetically, the last time I was here? The one handling the investigation of Salinas, the shakedown artist who had shot and wounded a shop owner, and so on and so forth?"

Giarrizzo, feeling a little like he was being made a fool of, gave him a dirty look. Then he said coldly:

"Now I remember. Go on."

"Salinas claimed he had an alibi, but didn't say what. You discovered that his defence would assert that at the moment that Alvarez was sh — "

"Good God! Who is Alvarez?"

"The shop owner wounded by Salinas. So, the defence would assert that Salinas, at that moment, was at the home of a certain Dolores, his mistress. And they were going to call Dolores's husband, and Dolores herself, to the witness box. You told me the prosecution maintained they could pick apart the alibi, but you yourself weren't absolutely certain. As it turns out, however, Inspector Martinez finds himself handling the case of a murdered man, who he discovers is a certain Pepito, a small-time crook working for the Mafia who also happened to be Dolores's husband."

"And who killed him?"

"Martinez assumes he was bumped off by a mafioso by the name of Bellavia — sorry, Sanchez. For some time now, Martinez has been asking himself why Dolores would agree to provide Salinas with an alibi. She certainly was not his mistress. So why would she do it? For money? Was she threatened? Was she coerced by violence? Then he has a brilliant idea. He goes to see Dolores at home, shows her the photo of the murdered Pepito, and tells her it was Sanchez who did it. At this point the woman has an unexpected reaction, which makes Martinez realize the incredible truth."

"Namely?"

"That Dolores did what she did for love."

"Love of whom?"

"Her husband. I repeat: it seems hard to believe, but it's true. Pepito is a scoundrel, he mistreats her, beats her, but she loves him and puts up with it all. Sanchez told her, meeting her alone: either you provide the alibi, or we kill Pepito, whom they've practically kidnapped. When Dolores learns from Martinez that he has been killed anyway, even though she has accepted the blackmail, she caves in, decides to avenge herself, and confesses. And there you have it."

He glanced at his watch.

"That took four and a half minutes," he said.

"All right, Montalbano, but, you see, Dolores confessed to a hypothetical police inspector who — "

"But she is ready to repeat everything to a concrete, non-hypothetical prosecutor. Shall we call this prosecutor by his proper name, Giarrizzo?"

"Then that changes everything. I'm going to call the carabinieri," said Giarrizzo, "and send them — "

"To the courtyard."

Giarrizzo balked.

"What courtyard?"

"The courthouse courtyard, right here. Mrs Siragusa — ah, sorry, I mean Dolores, is in one of my squad cars, under the escort of my chief sergeant Fazio. Martinez didn't want to leave her alone for even a second. Now that she's talked, she fears for her life. She's got a small suitcase with her, with her few personal effects. It should be easy for you, sir, to understand that the poor woman can no longer go home. They would bump her off in no time. Inspector Martinez hopes that Mrs Siragusa, sorry, I mean Dolores, will be protected as she deserves. Good day."

"Where are you going?"

"To the bar to eat a panino."

"So Licco is fucked, once and for all," said Fazio, when they were all back at the station.

"Right."

"Aren't you pleased?"

"No."

"Why not?"

"Because I didn't arrive at the truth until after many mistakes, too many."

"What mistakes?"

"I'll tell you just once, OK? Gurreri was never really taken on by the Mafia, as you put it, and as I put it to Giarrizzo, knowing it wasn't true. They merely held him hostage, letting him think they had taken him in. Whereas in fact he was constantly under the control of Ciccio Bellavia, who told him what he was supposed to do. And if his wife did not testify as they wanted her to do, they would kill him with no questions asked."

"So how does that change anything?"

"It changes everything, Fazio, everything. For example, stealing the horses. It could not have been Gurreri's idea. At most, he took part in the operation. That shoots down Lo Duca's hypothesis, which is that it was a vendetta on Gurreri's part. And now it's even less possible it was Gurreri who phoned Mrs Esterman."

"Maybe it was Bellavia?"

"Maybe, but I'm convinced that even Bellavia is doing somebody else's bidding. And I'm certain that of the two men who wanted to set fire to my house, the other one, the one who shot at Galluzzo, was Bellavia."

228

"So you think it's the Cuffaros who are behind all this."

"I no longer have any doubt. Augello was right when he said Gurreri's brain wasn't sharp enough to organize this kind of scheme, and you were right when you maintained that the Cuffaros wanted me to act a certain way at the trial. But they, too, have made a mistake. They have bothered the sleeping dog. And the dog, that is, me, has woken up and bitten them."

"Oh, Chief, I forgot to ask: how did Galluzzo take it?"

"Pretty well, all things considered. After all, he fired in self-defence."

"Sorry, but you told Concetta Siragusa that it was Bellavia who killed her husband?"

"As far as that goes, I told Prosecutor Giarrizzo the same thing."

"Fine, but we know he didn't do it."

"You have qualms about a criminal like Bellavia, who we know has got at least three murders under his belt? Three or four?"

"I don't have any qualms, Chief, but the guy's going to say he didn't do it."

"And who's going to believe him?"

"But what if he tells them what really happened? That it was someone from the police who shot Gurreri?"

"Then he'll have to tell them how and why. He'd have to say they came to my house to burn it down so I would act a certain way at the Licco trial. In other words he would have to bring the Cuffaros into the picture. Think he's going to want to do that?"

On the way back to Marinella, a wolf-like hunger assailed him. In the fridge he found a bowl of caponata whose scent filled the soul, and a plate of little wild asparagus, the kind that are bitter as poison, dressed only in olive oil and salt. In the oven was a loaf of wheat bread. He laid the table on the veranda and enjoyed himself. The night was pitch-black. A short distance from shore shone the lamp of a fishing boat. Seeing it there, he felt relieved, since he was now certain that nobody aboard the boat was spying on him.

He got into bed and started reading one of the Swedish books he had bought. Its protagonist was a colleague of his, Inspector Martin Beck, whose manner of investigation he found very appealing. When he had finished the novel and turned off the light, it was four o'clock in the morning.

As a result, he woke up at nine, but only because Adelina had made noise in the kitchen.

"Could you bring me a coffee, Adeli?"

"Iss ready, Isspector."

He drank it in little sips, savouring it, then lit a cigarette. When he finished it, he got up and went into the bathroom.

Later, all dressed and ready to go out, he went into the kitchen to have a second cup, as was his wont.

"Oh, signore, I gotta somethin f' you I keepa fuhgettin' a give you," said Adelina.

"What is it?"

"They gave itta me atta dry-cleaner when I went a get you' trousers. They foun' it inna pocket."

Her handbag was on a chair. She opened it, extracted something, and held it out to the inspector.

It was a horseshoe.

As the coffee was spilling onto his shirt, Montalbano felt the ground open up beneath his feet. Twice in twenty-four hours! It was really too much.

"Whass 'appenin', signore? You staina you' shirt."

He couldn't open his mouth. He kept staring, wide-eyed, at the horseshoe, benumbed, bewildered, flummoxed, and flabbergasted.

"Isspector, you make a me frighten! Whass' wrong?"

"Nothing, nothing," he managed to articulate.

He grabbed a glass, filled it with water, drank it down in one gulp.

"Nuthin', nuthin'," Adelina repeated, still looking at him, worried, with the horseshoe still in her hand.

"Give me that," he said, taking off his shirt. "And make me another pot of coffee."

"But isn't alla this coffee gonna make a you sick?"

He didn't answer. He drifted into the dining room as though sleepwalking and, still holding the horseshoe, picked up the receiver with one hand and dialled the number of the police station.

"Halloo! Vigàta Po — "

"Catarella, Montalbano here."

"Whass wrong, Chief? You got a weird voice!"

"Listen, I'm not coming in this morning. Is Fazio there?"

231

"No, sir, he in't onna premisses."

"Have him call me when he gets in."

He opened the French windows, went out on the veranda, sat down, laid the horseshoe on the table, and started staring at it as if he had never seen such a thing in his life. Slowly, he felt his brain resume functioning.

And the first thing that came back to him was the words of Dr Pasquano.

Montalbano, this is a clear sign of old age. A sign that your brain cells are disintegrating with increasing speed. The first symptom is memory loss. Did you know that? For example, does it sometimes happen that you'll do something one minute, and the next minute you'll forget that you did it?

It had happened. It had really happened! He had taken the horseshoe and put it in his pocket, forgetting completely about it. But when? And where?

"Here you' coffee, sir," said Adelina, setting a tray, with pot, cup, and sugar, on the table.

He drank a cup, scalding hot and bitter, while staring at the empty beach.

And all at once a dead horse appeared on the beach, lying on its side. And he saw himself belly down in front of the animal, reaching out and *touching a horseshoe almost completely detached from the hoof, held in place by a single nail sticking halfway out* . . .

And what happened next?

What happened was that something . . . something . . . Ah! That was it! Fazio, Gallo, and Galluzzo had appeared on the veranda, and he had stood up, slipping *the horseshoe mechanically into his pocket.*

232

Afterwards, he had gone to change his trousers, throwing them into the dirty-clothes hamper.

And after this, he had taken a shower, chatted with Fazio, and when the astronauts had arrived, the carcass was gone. *Keep your cool, Montalbà. You need another cup of coffee.*

So, let's start at the beginning. During the slaughter, the poor dying horse manages to escape, running desperately across the sand — *Good God! Want to bet that this was the track of sand in the bad dream he'd had? And that he had misinterpreted the dream?* — and ending up outside his window, where it collapses and dies. But its killers need to get rid of the carcass. So they get organized and come back with a handcart and a van, or small truck, or whatever. When they arrive a short while later to retrieve the carcass, they realize he has woken up, seen the horse, and come down onto the beach. And so they hide and wait for the right moment. Which comes when he and Fazio go into the kitchen, which has no windows facing the sea. They send a man out for reconnaissance. The man sees them in the kitchen, blithely chatting, and gives the others the go-ahead signal, all the while keeping his eye on him and Fazio. And in the twinkling of an eye, the carcass disappears. But then . . .

Was there another cup?

There wasn't any left in the pot, and he didn't have the courage to ask Adelina to make him another. So he stood up, went inside, grabbed a bottle of whisky and a glass, and turned to go back out on the veranda.

"First ting inna morning, Isspector?" came the voice of Adelina, who was standing in the kitchen doorway, watching him.

He froze. But he didn't answer her this time, either. He poured out the whisky and started to drink.

But then, if they were watching him when he was taking a close look at the animal, then they must have seen him take the horseshoe and put it in his pocket. Which meant that . . .

. . . you got it all wrong, Montalbà. All wrong.

They weren't trying to influence your behaviour at the Licco trial, Montalbà. The Licco trial doesn't have a damn thing to do with any of this.

They wanted the horseshoe. That was what they were looking for when they searched his house. And they had even returned his watch to let him know that it wasn't a case of burglary.

But why was the horseshoe so important?

The only logical answer was that as long as it was in his possession, it rendered the disappearance of the carcass useless.

But if it was so important, why, then, after the failed attempt at burning down his house, had they ceased trying?

Quite simple, Montalbà. Because Galluzzo had shot Gurreri, who then died. An unforeseen hitch. So surely they would be back, in one way or another.

He picked up the horseshoe again and started examining it. It was a perfectly normal horseshoe, like dozens of others he had seen.

234

What was so important about it that it should already have cost a man his life?

He raised his eyes to look out at the sea and was momentarily blinded by a flash of light. No, there wasn't anyone on a boat watching him through a pair of binoculars. The flash had gone off in his head.

He bolted upright, ran to the phone, and dialled Ingrid's number.

"Hillu? Who colling?"

"Is Rachele there?"

"You wait."

"Hello, who is this?"

"Montalbano here."

"Salvo! What a lovely surprise! I was just about to call you, you know. Ingrid and I thought of inviting you out to dinner tonight."

"All right, but — "

"Where would you like to go?"

"Come over to my place, you can be my guests. I'll ask Adelina to . . . But . . ."

"What are all these 'but's?"

"Tell me something. Your horse . . ."

"Yes?" said Rachele, expectant.

"Did your horse's shoes have anything unusual about them?"

"In what sense?"

"I don't know, I'm not very familiar with this sort of thing, as you know . . . Was there anything engraved in them, some sort of sign or symbol . . .?"

"Yes. Why do you want to know?"

"A silly idea of mine. What kind of symbol?"

"Right at the centre of the arch, on top, there is a small W, engraved in the metal. There's a blacksmith in Rome who makes them specially for me. His name is — "

"And does Lo Duca use the same smith for his — "

"Of course not!"

"Too bad," he said, appearing disappointed.

He hung up. He didn't want Rachele to start asking questions. The last piece of the puzzle that had first started to come together in his head on the evening in Fiacca had fallen into place and given a meaning to the whole scheme.

He started singing. Who was there to stop him? He broke into "Che gelida manina" in a loud voice.

"Signore! Signore! Wha'ss got inna you this morning?" asked the housekeeper, who had come running from the kitchen.

"Nothing, Adeli. Ah, listen. Make some good things for tonight. I've got two guests coming to dinner."

The phone rang. It was Rachele.

"We got cut off," the inspector said at once.

"Listen, what time do you want us to come?"

"Would nine o'clock be all right with you?"

"Nine is perfect. See you then."

He hung up and the telephone rang again.

"It's Fazio."

"No, no, I've changed my mind. I'm on my way there. Wait for me."

He sang all the way to the station. By this point he couldn't get those notes and words out of his head. And

236

when he reached the part where he couldn't remember them, he started over again from the top.

"*Se la lasci riscaldare . . .*"

He pulled up, got out, passed by Catarella, who, hearing him sing, sat there spellbound and open-mouthed.

"*Cercar che giova . . .* Cat, tell Fazio to come to my office straight away. *Se al buio non si trovaaa . . .*"

He went into his room, sat down, leaned back in his chair.

"*Ma per fortunaaa . . .*"

"What's happened, Chief?"

"Close the door, Fazio, and have a seat."

He took the horseshoe out of his pocket and set it down on the desk.

"Take a good look at it."

"Can I pick it up?"

"Sure."

As Fazio was studying the horseshoe, the inspector kept singing under his breath.

"*È una notte di luuuna . . .*"

Fazio gave him a questioning look.

"It's a perfectly ordinary horseshoe," he said.

"Exactly. And that's why they did everything within their power to get it back: they broke into my home, they tried to burn the place down, Gurreri lost his life . . ."

Fazio's eyes widened.

"All for this horseshoe . . .?"

"Yessirree."

"And you had it all the while."

"Yessirree. And I'd completely forgotten about it."

"But it's an ordinary horseshoe with no distinguishing characteristics!"

"And that is exactly what distinguishes it: the fact that it has no distinguishing characteristics."

"But what does that mean?"

"It means that the horse that was slaughtered did not belong to Rachele Esterman."

And he resumed in a low voice:

"*Vivo in povertà mia lieta . . .*"

CHAPTER
EIGHTEEN

Mimì Augello arrived late, and so the inspector had to repeat everything he had already told Fazio.

"All things considered, the horseshoe brought you good luck," was Augello's only comment. "It made you realize how things really stood."

Afterwards, Montalbano explained to both the idea he had in mind: to set up a complicated trap, an ambush, which would have to function like clockwork. And if all went well, they would haul in a net full of fish.

"Are you two in agreement?"

"Absolutely," said Mimì.

Fazio, for his part, seemed slightly doubtful.

"Chief, it's going to have to take place here, at the station, there's no question about that. The problem is that here, at the station, there's also Catarella."

"So what?"

"Chief, Catarella's liable to blow the whole thing for us. He's liable to bring Prestia into my office and Lo Duca into yours. You realize that with him around — "

"All right, have him come and see me. I'll send him on a secret mission. You, Fazio, make the phone calls you need to make, and then come back. You, too, Mimi, get organized."

The two went out, and a millionth of a second later, Catarella arrived on the run.

"Come in, Cat, lock the door, and sit down."

Catarella did as he was told.

"Now listen closely, because I'm going to give you a very delicate assignment that nobody else must know about. You mustn't whisper a word of this to anyone."

Getting excited, Catarella started squirming in his chair.

"I want you to go to Marinella and take up a position in a house under construction, just across the road from my house."

"I know the locality of the location, Chief. But whaddo I do after I take a position?"

"You must bring along a sheet of paper and a pen. I want you to take notes on every person who walks past my house along the beach. Write down if they're male, female, a child, and so on . . . When it gets dark, come back to the station with the list. Be sure not to let anyone see you! This is a top-secret matter. Now go."

Burdened with this tremendous responsibility, and moved to tears by the trust the inspector had placed in him, Catarella stood up, red as a turkeycock, and, unable to speak, gave a military salute, clicking his heels, then fumbled with the key in the lock, trying with great effort to open the door, which he finally did, and left.

240

"It's all done," said Fazio, returning after a brief spell. "Michilino Prestia will be here at four, and Lo Duca at four-thirty, on the dot. And here is Bellavia's address."

He handed him a little piece of paper, which Montalbano put in his pocket.

"Now I'm gonna go tell Gallo and Galluzzo what they're supposed to do," Fazio continued. "Inspector Augello told me to let them know that it's all set, and that he'll be ready in the car park at four o'clock."

"Good. You know what I say? I'm going to go and eat."

He pecked at some antipasti, decided against pasta, and forced himself to eat two sea bream. His stomach felt tight as a fist. And he no longer felt like singing. Without warning, apprehension about the afternoon's operation had come over him. Would it work?

"Inspector, you didn't do me justice today."

"Forgive me, Enzo, but today's just not the day."

He looked at his watch. There was just enough time for a stroll to the lighthouse, but not to sit down on the rock.

In Catarella's place there was Patrolman Lavaccara, a bright kid.

"Do you know what you have to do?"

"Yes, sir, Fazio explained it all to me."

The inspector went into his office, opened the window, smoked a cigarette, closed the window, and sat down at his desk. At that moment there was a knock at the door. It was ten minutes past four.

"Come in!"

Lavaccara appeared.

"Inspector, Mr Prestia is here."

"Show him in."

"Good afternoon, Inspector," said Prestia, entering.

As Lavaccara was closing the door and going back to his post, Montalbano stood up and held his hand out to Prestia.

"Please make yourself comfortable. I'm sincerely sorry to have bothered you, but you know how it is sometimes . . ."

Michele Prestia was over fifty, well dressed, with gold-rimmed spectacles and the air of an honest accountant. He looked completely calm.

"Give me about five minutes, and I'll be right with you."

He needed to stall. He pretended to be reading a document, every so often chuckling or knitting his eyebrows. Then he set it aside and stared at Prestia a long time without saying anything. Fazio had said that Prestia was a nobody, a rag doll in Bellavia's hands. He appeared, however, to have nerves of steel. At last the inspector made up his mind.

"Your wife has filed a report with us. Against you."

Prestia balked. He blinked a few times. Perhaps, being already in with the wrong crowd, he was expecting something else. He opened and closed his mouth a few times before managing to speak.

"My wife?!! Reported me?!"

242

"She wrote us a long letter."

"My wife?!"

He couldn't get over the shock.

"And what does she accuse me of?"

"Continuous abuse."

"Me?! So I supposedly — "

"Mr Prestia, I advise you not to keep denying the fact."

"But this is insane! I've stumbled into a nuthouse! May I see the letter?"

"No. We've already sent it to the prosecutor."

"Look, Inspector, there's clearly been some kind of mistake here. I — "

"Are you Michele Prestia?"

"Yes."

"Fifty-five years old?"

"No, sir. Fifty-three."

Montalbano wrinkled his brow, as though suddenly prey to doubt.

"Are you sure about that?"

"Absolutely!"

"Hmph. Do you live at Via Lincoln 47?"

"No, I live at Via Abate Meli 32."

"Really? Could I see some identification, please?"

Prestia took out his wallet and handed him his ID card, which Montalbano studied very long and carefully. Every so often he looked up at Prestia, then back down at the document.

"It seems clear to me that — " Prestia began.

"Nothing is clear. Excuse me a moment. I'll be right back."

He stood up, left the room, closed the door, and went to see Lavaccara. With him in Catarella's cupboard was also Galluzzo, waiting for him.

"Is he here yet?"

"Yes, sir. I just brought him to Fazio," said Lavaccara.

"Galluzzo, come with me."

He went back into his office, followed by Galluzzo and wearing an expression of mortification. He left the door open.

"I am terribly sorry, Mr Prestia. This is a case of mistaken identity. I beg your pardon for any trouble I may have caused you. Go with Corporal Galluzzo, who will have you sign your release. Good day."

He held out his hand to him. Prestia muttered something and left the room, preceded by Galluzzo. Montalbano felt himself turn into a statue. This was the critical moment. Prestia took two steps into the corridor and found himself face to face with Lo Duca, who was coming out of Fazio's office in turn, followed by Fazio himself. Montalbano saw the two men freeze for a moment, paralysed. Galluzzo had a sudden flash of genius and said, cop-like:

"Let's go, Prestia! Keep moving!"

Prestia resumed walking. Fazio lightly shoved Lo Duca, who was in a daze. Their strategy was working perfectly.

"Chief, Mr Lo Duca is here," said Fazio.

"Come in, come in. And you can stay, Fazio, if you like. Please make yourself comfortable, Mr Lo Duca."

Lo Duca sat down. He was pale and clearly had not recovered from having seen Prestia come out of the inspector's office.

"I do not understand why you have so rashly — "

"I'll tell you in a minute. But first I must ask you officially: Mr Lo Duca, do you want a lawyer?"

"No! Why should I need a lawyer?"

"As you wish. Mr Lo Duca, I have summoned you here because I need to ask you some questions concerning the stolen horses."

Lo Duca gave a tense smile.

"Oh, for that? Go right ahead."

"The evening we spoke to each other, in Fiacca, you told me that the theft of the horses, and the killing of the one we presumed to be Mrs Esterman's, was a vendetta on the part of a certain Gerlando Gurreri, whom you, a few years ago, had struck with an iron bar, permanently disabling him. Which was why the lady's horse was bludgeoned to death with iron bars. A sort of tit for tat, if I remember correctly."

"Yes . . . I think I said something like that."

"Excellent. Who was it that told you, Mr Lo Duca, that the horse was killed by iron bars?"

Lo Duca looked disoriented.

"Well . . . I think it was Rachele Esterman . . . or maybe somebody else. But why does it matter?"

"It matters, Mr Lo Duca. Because I never told Mrs Esterman how her horse was killed. And nobody else could have known; I only told one other person, someone who has no relations with you."

"But this is a minor point which — "

"Which triggered my first suspicion. You, I must admit, were very shrewd that evening. You played a subtle game. You not only gave me Gurreri's name, but you even expressed doubt that the slaughtered horse was Rachele Esterman's."

"Listen, Inspector —"

"No, you listen to me. A second suspicion was triggered when I learned from Mrs Esterman that you had insisted her horse be kept in your stable."

"But that was a simple courtesy!"

"Mr Lo Duca, before you go any further, I should warn you that I've just had a long and fruitful conversation with Michele Prestia. Who, in exchange for a certain, well, benevolence on our part towards him, has given me some precious information on the theft of the horses."

Touché! Bull's-eye! Lo Duca turned even paler, started sweating, and squirmed in his chair. He had seen, with his own eyes, Prestia come out after talking to the inspector, and he had heard him being treated roughly by another policeman. He therefore believed the lie. But he tried nevertheless to defend himself.

"I have no idea what that individual might have — "

"Allow me to continue. And guess what? I finally found what you were looking for."

"What *I* was looking for? And what was that?"

"This," said Montalbano.

He reached into his pocket, pulled out the horseshoe, and set it down on the desk. It was the *coup de grâce*. Lo Duca teetered so severely, he risked falling out of his chair. A string of spittle trickled from his open mouth. He realized he was finished.

"This is a perfectly ordinary horseshoe, with no distinguishing marks. I removed it myself from the hoof of the dead horse. The shoes of Mrs Esterman's horse, on the other hand, had a little W on them. Who could have been aware of this detail? Certainly not Prestia or Bellavia, or the late lamented Gurreri; but you, sir, you were aware of it. And you alerted your accomplices. And so, aside from the carcass, you absolutely needed to retrieve the horseshoe as well, which I had taken. Because that shoe, you see, could prove that the slaughtered horse was not the lady's — as you wanted everyone to believe — but yours, which was, among other things, very sick and would shortly be put down. Just now Prestia explained to me that a horse like Esterman's would bring in millions to the organizers of the illegal horse-racing circuit. But you, I'm sure, didn't do it for money. So why, then? Were you being blackmailed?"

Lo Duca, who could no longer speak and was drenched in sweat, dropped his head and nodded. Then he drew as much breath as he could and said:

"They wanted one of my horses for the illegal races, and when I refused . . . they showed me a photo . . . of me . . . with a little boy."

"That's enough, Mr Lo Duca. I'll take it from here. So, since Mrs Esterman's horse bore a great resemblance to one of yours, which was soon to die, you came up with the plan of the bogus theft and the bloody slaughter of your horse, so that it would look like a vendetta. But how could you have the heart to do it?"

Lo Duca buried his face in his hands. Big teardrops started seeping through his fingers.

"I was desperate . . . I ran off to Rome so I wouldn't have to . . ."

"All right," said Montalbano. "Listen to me. It's over. I'll ask you one more question, and then you're free to go."

"Free . . .?"

"I'm not in charge of this investigation. You filed your report at Montelusa Central, no? Therefore I'm leaving the matter up to your conscience. You act as you think best. But take my advice: you must go and confess everything to my colleagues in Montelusa. They'll try to keep the business of the photograph under wraps, I'm sure of it. If you don't do this, you will be surrendering yourself, bound hand and foot, to the Cuffaros, who will squeeze you like a lemon and then throw you away. So my question is this: do you know where Prestia is hiding Mrs Esterman's horse?"

This question, as Montalbano knew all too well, was the one weak point in the whole architecture he had constructed. If Prestia had actually talked, he would certainly have also told him where the horse was being kept. But Lo Duca was too upset, too annihilated, to notice what a strange question it was.

"Yes," he said.

Fazio had to help Lo Duca rise from his chair, and then walked him to his car, holding him up all the while.

"But are you up to driving?"

"Y . . . yes."

He watched the car drive off after nearly crashing into another, and then went back to the inspector's office.

"What do you think? Will he go to the Montelusa police?"

"I think so. Call Augello and pass me the phone."

Mimì answered at once.

"Are you following Prestia?"

"Yes. He's heading towards Siliana."

"Mimì, we've just learned that he's hiding the horse about two and a half miles past Siliana, at a stable in the country. And I'm sure he's left someone on guard there. How many men have you got with you?"

"Four in a Jeep and two in a little van."

"Stay on the alert, Mimì. And if anything happens, call Fazio."

He hung up.

"Is the car with Gallo and Galluzzo ready?"

"Yes, sir."

"All right, then, you stay here, in my office. Tell Lavaccara to put all calls through to you. We'll report back to you. Repeat the address to me, I can't find it."

"Via Crispi 10. It's a ground-floor office with two rooms. The bodyguard's in the first room. And he's always in the second — that is, when he's not out killing someone."

"Gallo, let's get one thing straight. And this time, mind you, I'm serious. I don't want any sirens or screeching tyres. We have to catch him by surprise. And I don't want you to pull up at number 10, but a little before."

"But won't you be with us, Chief?"

"No, I'll follow you in my car."

It took them about ten minutes to get there. Montalbano parked behind the squad car and got out. Galluzzo came up to him.

"Chief, Fazio ordered me to tell you to get your gun."

"I'm getting it."

He opened the glove compartment, grabbed the weapon, and put it in his pocket.

"Gallo, you stay behind in the first room and keep an eye on the guard. You, Galluzzo, are coming with me into the second room. There's no way out at the back, so he can't escape. I'll go in first. And I mean it: as little racket as possible."

It was a short street, and there were about ten cars parked in it. There were no shops. A man and a dog were the only living things visible.

Montalbano went in. A man of about thirty was sitting behind a desk reading the sports pages. He looked up, saw Montalbano, recognized him, and sprang to his feet, opening his jacket with his right hand to reach for a revolver he had tucked into his belt.

"Don't do anything stupid," said Gallo in a low voice, pointing his gun at him.

The man put his hand on the desk. Montalbano and Galluzzo looked at one another, and then the inspector turned the knob of the door to the second room and opened it, going in with Galluzzo following behind.

"Ah!" said a bald man of about fifty in shirtsleeves, with a shifty-looking face and slits for eyes, setting down the telephone receiver he had in his hand. He didn't seem the least bit surprised.

"I am Inspector Montalbano."

"I know you well, Inspector. And him, aren't you going to introduce him to me?" he said ironically, never taking his eyes off Galluzzo. "I have the feeling I've seen this gentleman before."

"Are you Francesco Bellavia?"

"Yes."

"You are under arrest. And I should warn you that whatever you say in your defence, nobody will believe you."

"That's not the right formula," said Bellavia, who started laughing.

Then he calmed down and said: "Don't worry, Galluzzo, I won't say I killed Gurreri, but I won't say you killed him, either. So why are you arresting me?"

"For the theft of two horses."

Bellavia started laughing even harder.

"You can imagine how scared I am! And what's your proof?"

"Lo Duca and Prestia have confessed," said Montalbano.

"A fine pair, those two! One goes with little children, and the other is a doormat!"

He got up and held out his wrists for Galluzzo.

"Go on, handcuff me yourself! That way the farce is complete!"

Without looking into Bellavia's eyes, which were boring into him, Galluzzo put the handcuffs on him.

"Where are we taking him?"

"To Prosecutor Tommaseo. When you set off for Montelusa, I'll tell him you're on your way."

He returned to headquarters and went into his office.

"Any news?" he asked Fazio.

"Nothing yet. What about you?"

"We've arrested Bellavia. He didn't put up any resistance. I'm going to call Tommaseo from Mimì's office."

The prosecutor was still at his desk. He protested, reproaching the inspector for not telling him a thing about the case.

"It all happened in the space of a few hours, sir. There was simply no time whatsoever to — "

"And you arrested him on what charge?"

"The theft of two horses."

"Well, for a figure like Bellavia it's a pretty paltry charge."

"You know what they say where I come from, sir? That every bit of fly shit counts. Anyway, I'm sure it was Bellavia who killed Gurreri. If we work him hard enough, and he's a tough one, he'll end up admitting to something."

He went back into his office and found Fazio on the telephone.

"Yes . . . yes . . . All right. I'll relay that to the chief."

He set down the receiver and said to Montalbano:

252

"Inspector Augello told me they saw Prestia go into a house that has a stable next to it. But since there are four cars, apart from Prestia's, parked outside, Augello thinks there may be a meeting going on. He wants to avoid a shoot-out: says it's better to wait for the others to leave."

"He's right."

A good hour went by without any phone calls coming in. Apparently it was a long meeting. Montalbano couldn't wait any longer.

"Call Mimì and ask him what's happening."

Fazio spoke to Augello.

"He says they're still inside, and there are at least eight of them. It's best to wait a little longer."

Montalbano glanced at his watch and leapt to his feet. It was already eight-thirty.

"Listen, Fazio, I absolutely have to go to Marinella. As soon as there's any news, ring me."

He raced home, opened the French windows, and laid the table on the veranda.

He had barely finished when the doorbell rang. He went to open the door. There were Ingrid and Rachele, loaded down with three bottles of wine, two of whisky, and a parcel.

"It's a cassata," Ingrid explained.

So they had serious intentions. Montalbano went into the kitchen to uncork the bottles when he heard the phone ring. It must be Fazio.

"One of you get that!" he said.

He heard Rachele's voice say:

"Hello?"

Then:

"Yes, this is the home of Inspector Montalbano. Who is this?"

He suddenly had an inkling that sent chills down his spine. He dashed into the dining room. Rachele had just put down the receiver.

"Who was it?"

"A woman. She didn't say her name. She hung up."

He didn't sink underground like the other times, but felt the ceiling come crashing down on his head. Surely that was Livia who had called! And now how was he going to explain to her that it was a perfectly innocent gathering? Damn the moment when he decided to invite them to dinner! He foresaw a bitter night ahead, spent mostly on the telephone. Chagrined, he returned to the kitchen, and the phone rang again.

"I'll get it! I'll get it!" he yelled.

This time it was Fazio.

"Chief? It's all done. Inspector Augello has arrested Prestia and is taking him to the prosecutor's. They've recovered Esterman's horse. It appears to be in excellent shape. They've put it into the van."

"Where are they taking it?"

"To the stable of a friend of Inspector Augello's. Augello has also informed Montelusa of everything."

"Thanks, Fazio. We've really done a very fine job."

"It was all your doing, Chief,"

He went out on the veranda. Leaning against the French windows, he said to the two women: "After we've eaten, I have something to tell you."

254

He didn't want to ruin the meal that was waiting for him with the tremendous bother of hugs, tears, emotions, and thanks.

"Let's go and see what Adelina has prepared for us," he said.

Author's Note

As with all the other novels with Inspector Montalbano as protagonist, the present one was suggested to me by two news items: a horse found slaughtered on a beach near Catania, and the theft of two horses from a stable in Grosseto province, in Tuscany.

By this point I think it useless to say — but I'll do so anyway — that the names of the characters and the situations in which they find themselves have been entirely invented by me, and therefore have no connection whatsoever with any actual, living persons.

Should anyone happen to recognize him- or herself in this story, it means only that they have a better imagination than I do.

Notes

page 17 — **all the *vocumprà* in the province**: *vocumprà* are the foreign pedlars, usually of North African or sub-Saharan origin, that one often encounters on the streets of today's Italy. The name is derived from the question *Vuoi comprare?* or *Vuole comprare?* (Do you want to buy?), which they shorten to *Vocumprà* (sometimes to *Vucumprà*), an abbreviation also redolent of the Neapolitan and Roman dialects, which may be where they first picked it up.

page 21 — **The bright-eyed goddess** . . . : a common epithet for the Greek goddess Pallas Athena.

page 33 — ***cipuddrata***: Sicilian for *cipollata*, that is, onion sauce.

page 49 — **"No, Vario's his given name"**: in Italian bureaucratic usage, the surname is always placed before the first name, giving rise to some confusion in cases such as the present one, Vario Ippolito, where both names could be first names.

page 76 — ... **wearing an expression fit for All Souls' Day**: in Italy, as in the Spanish-speaking world, All Souls' Day (2 November, immediately following All Saints' Day) is called the Day of the Dead, and commemorates the faithful departed. The Sicilian expression used by Camilleri actually translates literally as "a November-the-second face".

page 98 — **Quartetto Cetra**: the Quartetto Cetra, also known as I Cetra, were a popular Italian vocal quartet in the 1940s who performed for the stage and eventually, in the 1950s, for television. The Visconte di Castelfrombone and the Duca di Lomantò were two characters in their often satirical songs and skits.

page 99 — **It was like the ending of a tragic film**: namely *Viaggio in Italia* (*Journey to Italy*, 1954), starring Ingrid Bergman and George Sanders, a moving tale of a doomed love relationship, the closing image of which has Bergman's character being swept away by a moving throng of Neapolitans from her estranged husband, played by Sanders.

page 111 — ... **having been first with that twenty-year-old girl, whose name he did not even want to remember**: see Andrea Camilleri, *August Heat*, Macmillan, 2009.

page 122 — **"We'll go and visit the temples"**: the model for the fictional town of Montelusa is the city of Agrigento (Girgenti in Sicilian), which was a major

Greek centre (Akragas) in antiquity. Seven monumental temples in the Doric style survive in what is known as the "Valley of the Temples", just outside of modern Agrigento.

page 173 — **Shrimps, langoustine, flying squid, smoked tuna, fried balls of *nunnatu*, sea urchins, mussels, clams, octopus morsels** a *strascinasale*, **octopus morsels** affucati, **tiny fried squid, squid and cuttlefish tossed in a salad with orange slices and celery, capers wrapped in anchovies, sardines** a beccafico, **swordfish carpaccio** ... : nunnatu (Sicilian for neonato, or "new-born") are tiny new-born fish, available only at certain times of the year. Octopus a strascinasale is simply boiled in salted water and dressed with olive oil and lemon juice; and affucati means "drowned", in this case in a classic Sicilian tomato-sauce base for seafood. Sardines a beccafico is a Sicilian speciality named after a small bird, the beccafico (Sylvia borin, the garden warbler), which is particularly fond of figs (beccafico means "fig-pecker"). The headless, cleaned sardines are stuffed with sautéed bread crumbs, pine nuts, sultanas, and anchovies, then rolled up so that they resemble the bird when they come out of the oven.

page 176 — *Madamina, il catalogo è questo:* literally, "Here is the list, little lady." The famous catalogue aria from Mozart's opera Don Giovanni, in which Leporello, Don Giovanni's servant, enumerates and describes his master's many female conquests.

page 191 — **Fangio on the Carrera Panamericana**: Juan Manuel Fangio (1911–95) of Argentina was a famous racing driver who dominated Formula One for much of his career. He won the Carrera Panamericana in 1953.

page 201 — **the horse . . . was made of bronze and half collapsed, sitting on its haunches, just like the RAI horse**: the symbol of the RAI (Radiotelevisione Italiana, the national, state-owned radio and television network) is as described, and there is a bronze statue of it outside the network offices. The author worked for many years directing television and stage productions for the network.

page 236 — **He broke into "Che gelida manina" in a loud voice**: a famous scene from Act I of Puccini's opera *La Bohème* (1896), sung by Rodolfo, the destitute poet and male lead, to Mimì, the beautiful seamstress and lead female role, when the girl loses her key in the dark during a visit to the poet's garret, and he helps her to look for it. I quote below the first half of the aria, the part from which Montalbano sings a few lines (and not always correctly). I have provided a translation for the non-Italian reader of the passage from which the inspector sings.

> *Che gelida manina,*
> *se la lasci riscaldar.*
> *Cercar che giova?*
> *Al buio non si trova.*

Ma per fortuna
è una notte di luna,
e qui la luna
l'abbiamo vicina.
Aspetti, signorina,
le dirò con due parole
chi son, e che faccio,
come vivo. Vuole?
Chi son? Sono un poeta.
Che cosa faccio? Scrivo.
E come vivo? Vivo.
In povertà mia lieta
scialo da gran signore
rimi e inni d'amore.

[What a cold little hand,
let me warm it for you.
Why bother to search?
We won't find it in the dark,
But luckily
it is a moonlit night
and we have the moon
near us tonight.
Wait, signorina,
I will tell you in two words
who I am, what I do,
and how I live. Shall I?
Who am I? I am a poet.
What do I do? I write.
How do I live? I live.
In my happy poverty

like a great lord
I lavish rhymes and hymns of love . . .]

Notes by Stephen Sartarelli

Other titles published by Ulverscroft:

THE TREASURE HUNT

Andrea Camilleri

When a letter arrives containing a mysterious riddle, Inspector Montalbano becomes drawn into a perplexing treasure hunt set by an anonymous challenger. As the hunt intensifies, Montalbano is offered assistance from Arturo Pennisi, a young man eager to witness the detective's investigative skills first hand. Fending off meddling commissioners and his irate girlfriend, Livia, the inspector will follow the treasure hunt's clues and travel from Vigàta's teeming streets to its deserted outskirts. But when a horrifying crime is committed, the game must surely be laid aside. And it isn't long before Montalbano himself will be in terrible danger . . .

THE DANCE OF THE SEAGULL

Andrea Camilleri

Inspector Montalbano is sitting on his porch at dawn, when a seagull falls from the sky, performing a strange dance, before lying down to die. Perplexed by what he has witnessed, the scene hangs over him like an omen. About to depart for a holiday, Montalbano makes a quick trip to the police station to tie up loose ends. But when his dear colleague Fazio is discovered missing — and it transpires that the policeman had been involved in his own secret investigations — Montalbano instead launches a desperate search for his lost friend, as time begins to run out . . .

THE AGE OF DOUBT

Andrea Camilleri

The day after a storm, Inspector Montalbano encounters a strange woman who expresses interest in a certain yacht scheduled to dock that afternoon. Not long after she's gone, the yacht's crew reports finding a disfigured corpse. Also at anchor is a luxury vessel with a somewhat shady crew. Both boats will have to stay in Vigàta until the investigation is over and, based on information from the woman, Montalbano begins to think the occupants of the yacht might know more about the man's death than they're letting on.

MYSTERY IN THE CHANNEL

Freeman Wills Crofts

1931: The *Chichester* is making a routine journey across the English Channel on a pleasant afternoon in June, when the steamer's crew spot a small yacht bobbing aimlessly in the water. Upon boarding the vessel, they discover two male corpses. Both must have been shot, but there is no sign of either the murderer or the pistol. Inspector French is put on the case, and soon establishes the identity of the dead men: Moxon and Deeping, the top dogs at one of the largest financial houses in the UK. What's more, the firm is on the brink of collapse. One and a half million pounds has gone missing, along with Moxon and Deeping, who seem to have been fleeing the country with their ill-gotten gains. So who killed them, and how?